Also by John Cady

<u>Novels</u>
Angela of Death
Angela of Death II – Iron Sharpens Iron
(Available Sep. 2024)

<u>Novellas</u>
Attack of the 3-D Zombies

<u>Anthology Contributions</u>
"The Inker" (*The Killer Collection*)
"Our House" (*Books of Horror Anthology*)
"A Lesson on the Trail" (*Horror USA: Washington*)
"Nurse Kerrie: Monster Whisperer" (*Flashes of Hope*)
"Thomson's America" (*After the Kool-Aid is Gone*)
"Late to the Party" (*Holiday Horror Book 5: Dark Halloween*)
"Disappearance to the Dark Realm" (*Dark Magic*)
"Crushed" (*Drabbles of Dread Anthology*)
"Squatters Rights" (*Drabbles of Dread Anthology*)
"Wedge War: The Aftermath" (*It's All Fun and Games Until Someone Dies*)
"Vessel" (*Supernatural Drabbles of Dread*)
"Spirited Away" (*Supernatural Drabbles of Dread*)
"The Steepest Fare" (*Night Terrors – Scare Street*)
"Y is for Yarn" (*ABC's of Terror – Vol. 3*)
"A Demonic Dip" (*Trapped - Gravestone Press*)
"Nullus Ingredior" (*Mermaids - Iron Faerie Publishing*)
"A Taste of Aries" (*The Dire Circle Anthology*)
"Mom's Tree" (*Jersey Pines Ink Trees Anthology*)
"A Loner's Best Friend" (*Ctrl Alt Del Anthology*)
"The Finisher" (*Ctrl Alt Del Anthology*)
"The Assassin's Sidecar" (*Steampunk Anthology – Iron Fairie*)

Angela of Death

John Cady

Published by Watertower Hill Publishing, LLC

Cover and internal artwork by Susan Roddey at The Snark Shop by Phoenix and Fae Creations.
Copyright © 2024 Watertower Hill Publishing LLC.

Author's Note
All character and names in this book are fictional and are not designed, patterned after, nor descriptive of any person, living or deceased.
Any similarities to people, living or deceased is purely by coincidence. Author and Publisher are not liable for any likeness described herein.

Library of Congress Control Number:

Paperback ISBN:
Hardback ISBN: 979-8-9893011-9-5
eBook AISN: B0CS3X3NY5

Published in the United States of America
19 17 15 13 11 9 7 5 3 1

This book is dedicated to my amazing wife, who is as beautiful inside as she is outside, and my incredible children, who make me proud every single day.

"A hero is someone who has given his or her life to something bigger than oneself."

- Joseph Campbell

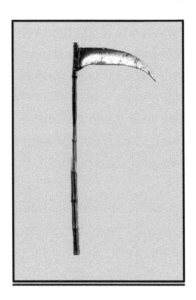

<u>Chapter 1</u>
Angela

They brought me out to a grassy field I hadn't stepped foot on since I last played munchkin soccer there; I was the smallest girl on the field then, and nothing had changed.

I stood in the center of a circle they had formed, just waiting for the first girl to lunge at me. I kept my eyes straight ahead, focusing mostly on Kiki. This wasn't because she was the toughest of the girls; it was simply because there really wasn't any point in being aware of my surroundings. They were *all* going to beat me down regardless. I needed them to.

It was the first stage in my initiation; I needed to be jumped in by the other Destinas.

The deal was they beat me down for two straight minutes, during which time I couldn't defend myself. If I even tried to, they were going to start all over again. It was either go with this or let a few, if not all, of the Destinos have their way with me.

1

It literally would have come down to a roll of the dice, too; wherein if I rolled a two, I needed to have sex with two of them and so on and so forth. Let's just say two was the best-case scenario.

I felt good about my choice. Cuts and bruises heal after a while.

The Destinas started back when my mother was a teenager. She herself never joined, but they looked out for her because she looked the other way for them. She wasn't proud of this, but I don't think she had much of a choice.

Anyways, how they came up with the name was simple enough; a destina (aside from being another word for destiny) was basically the most superior type of female on the earth; she was far prettier and far more intelligent than anyone you compared her with.

I felt the first punch connect with the back of my head and then it was on; I *was* able to brace myself for that first shot, so I don't think she did as much damage as she was hoping for. I knew where it was coming from because I saw Kiki's eyes move from mine to whoever she could see over my right shoulder, and I knew my head was the target because it's the first part of the body everyone aims for.

I was able to stay on my feet for a little while, but they quickly brought me to the ground and rained Timbs down on me.

"No more head shots, Rosa!" One of the girls shouted, just as the sole of a Timb was coming down at my face.

It stopped halfway down, and Rosa barely managed to keep her balance.

"I think Angela's had enough."

I was still numb when they helped me to my feet – one under each arm. Aside from any further kicks to the head, I'm pretty sure they held nothing back.

For my troubles, I received a hug and a kiss upon my right cheek from each of them. The final girl to embrace me was Lucia; she was the

2

head Destina. She was the one who gave Rosa the order to lay off of my head.

"Am I in?" I asked.

This, of course, was naïve of me.

"Not yet," she laughed.

"There's one more thing you need to do before you can call yourself a Destina. Sorry to break it to you, but this was only stage one, girl. Your loyalty test is the biggie; complete that, and you're in. Meet us at Kiki's tonight. Nine o'clock."

I cleaned myself up when I got home. Luckily, my mother wasn't there to see what I looked like. I could barely bring *myself* to look in the mirror.

I tried to convince myself it was an honor to wear these cuts and bruises – that they meant something special, they were supposed to be a symbol of belonging. The scars they left were supposed to be some sort of a road map to my destiny.

At least, this was how they explained them. Still, even with this outlook, it wasn't easy seeing them.

On my way to the front door, I passed by my mother's rocking chair. She sat there whenever she read. Her book of choice most nights was the Bible.

In fact, it was right there resting on the cushion.

That thing was worn out. Let me tell you. It had looked that way for as long as I could remember. It was just like the ones at our church. Maybe they let her keep it. Maybe that's how she got it. Churches are generous like that sometimes.

I used to pretend to read it all the time when I was a kid. I could get away with it because the priest was reading it aloud anyways. I just listened to him. I don't think it made a difference. As long as I knew what passage he was discussing, that's all that mattered.

Mama didn't seem to mind. She was probably just happy I wasn't talking during the mass. That was her pet peeve.

I said a little prayer before I left for Kiki's. I figured I could use all the help I could get that night and all the nights that followed - especially since I'd be joining a gang. I needed a little added protection.

Mama worked long hours to support me, so I was already well on my way to Kiki's by the time she was probably pulling into the driveway. I could try to explain my cuts and bruises to her in the morning.

Most nights, I wished she didn't have to work so late, but I welcomed it that night; I was glad she didn't have to see me.

Kiki's house was dimly lit. Other than the cars in the driveway, there was no indication whatsoever that anyone was there; they didn't even leave the television on in the living room, and that thing always seemed to be on.

My mother would have killed me if I had wasted that much juice.

I was about to knock on the front door when I received a text message from Kiki. It read: "Where you at, girl? Just walk right in and come downstairs when you get here."

I didn't reply. Instead, I just followed her directions.

When I found them down there, they had all surrounded one girl who was kneeling in the center of the room – eyes on the floor. Her name was Lil' Marie. She was the one who probably hit me the hardest.

Everyone looked pissed; I wondered what she had done. Lucia looked the angriest. In fact, she didn't even acknowledge me for the first few minutes I was there.

All she did was pace back and forth before Lil' Marie, and then slowly began circling her like a shark. This wasn't good.

"They're our rivals, Lil' Marie!" Lucia shouted. "Our enemies!"

"Look, I'm sorry," Lil' Marie apologized, sobbing uncontrollably.

Even as she apologized she didn't make eye contact with Lucia. I'm not sure I would have either; Lucia was giving her the daggers. I'd never seen her eyes with that much anger behind them. Then again, based on their exchange, I guess she should have been pissed.

4

"Sorry?" Lucia shouted. "You could have gotten us killed! You've left us no choice."

Lucia shrugged her shoulders. Lil' Marie finally glanced up at her with fear in her eyes – more fear than I'm willing to bet they'd ever shown. That's when I realized the severity of Lucia's decision.

"No! Please, Lucia!" Lil' Marie pleaded, shaking her head. "There has to be another way!"

I really wanted there to be another way. I didn't want to witness what I thought was coming. Lucia simply stood there, arms crossed and shaking her head.

I could see the barrel of a nine poking out from under her top arm. What was I getting myself into? *What the hell was I getting myself into?* It was getting a little too real now.

"Angela!" Lucia shouted, completely catching me off guard. What did she want with me?

Then, it dawned on me: my loyalty test. *Ay Dios mio. Oh, please God, don't let this be it,* was my only thought.

"Yes?" I reluctantly answered. Something told me I didn't want to keep her waiting too long.

She unfolded her arms, readied the nine, and held it out for me to take. She shook it a little when I didn't grab it quickly enough – that alone was enough to make me nervous.

"She's a traitor," she said. "There's only one way to deal with a traitor. Get her right in the back of the head, close range."

I grabbed hold of the gun. It was much heavier than the ones they used in the movies looked. Granted, those were all probably fakes, loaded with blanks. I felt smaller than ever. These girls I grew up with suddenly seemed a lot older than me.

I stared down at the gun in my tiny hand, which had always seemed big enough prior to this moment. I can't even tell you I backed out at the last second because I didn't get that far; I chickened out pretty much right away.

"I can't," I said. "I'm sorry. I really thought I was for this. I'm… I'm not, though."

I looked down at the back of Lil' Marie's head, trying to imagine what it would have been like pulling the trigger, but, alas, I couldn't even do that. I simply couldn't take a life; it wasn't in me.

And here I was all this time, *pretending* to be some tough Chicana. I honestly thought I was Destina material. I wasn't, though.

Lucia looked disappointed as she held her hand out. Even though my face most likely didn't express this, I was more than happy to give it back to her. It was very out of place in my little hand.

She nonchalantly aimed the nine at Lil' Marie's head and pulled the trigger. It was much louder than it seemed in the movies.

I quickly looked away, expecting to hear the limp body fall to the floor. When I didn't, I glanced up into the eyes of the girl standing closest to me; she smirked, probably having known all along I didn't have it in me.

She motioned for me to turn around; I really didn't want to see what was left of Lil' Marie, but I suppose I had no choice.

When I finally did turn back around, Lucia was helping her to her feet. She wasn't dead; she wasn't even hurt. *Blanks*.

I'd been duped by the Destinas. It was just what she told me it would be: a test. And I failed. I glanced down at the floor in disgust.

Luckily, I didn't cry because this only would have made things worse.

Lucia handed the nine (if it even was a real nine) to Lil' Marie, and then approached me. She placed the tip of her index finger beneath my chin and tilted my head back until I couldn't help but stare directly into her eyes.

They still looked disappointed, but she surprised me when she pulled me in for a hug and released me a few seconds later.

"It's okay, Angela," she said. "If you're not for it, then you're not for it. You're just like your mother, which is a *good* thing, girl. She's a

6

good woman, and she's always been good to me. Honestly, I was surprised and maybe even a little disappointed when you first told me you wanted to join. I told myself, 'This isn't her.' Now, I see I was right. To keep it a hundred, I even gave you more to do, hoping you wouldn't wanna put up with it, but here you are."

"What do you mean?" I asked.

She smirked.

"None of the other girls needed to take a 'loyalty test.' They got jumped in, and that was it."

"That's not fair," I said, not exactly too beaten up over it, though, pardon the pun.

"I'm hip," she admitted.

"And I'm sorry, but it was for your own good. Like you yourself said, you ain't for this. Everyone else here probably would have pulled that trigger."

"Well, I'm sorry I wasted your time," I apologized. "Actually, I'm sorry I wasted everyone's time."

I scanned the room. None of them seemed upset with me; they were all following Lucia's lead. Even if they were pissed off, I guess they knew better than to show it.

"Hey, don't worry about it," Lucia said. "They'll get over it. And I think I would've been a little heartbroken if you had actually pulled that trigger. I need an amiga who isn't Destina. We all do. Right, girls?"

I scanned the room again. They all nodded.

"Si," Lil' Marie added.

"I'm Destina for life," Lucia began. "But they're not all I need. You got that?"

I did. I nodded, smiling.

"Good," she said, smiling herself. "You do have to go now, though, because we have some things to discuss that aren't for your ears."

"I understand," I said. Then I turned and made for the stairs.

I wasn't even halfway down her front steps before I heard the shots. Drive-by.

I'm still not sure who it was; perhaps the Rivers Street Girlz. They were the Destinas' rivals. Thankfully, none of the Destinas were hit; they were all still down in the basement.

I, on the other hand, was most likely dead before I hit the ground.

When I awoke, I was seated on the steps, looking down at my blood-splattered body. My eyes were wide open. I tried to count how many times they got me.

A man's voice broke my concentration, though. He was seated to my right; I hadn't even noticed him. I suppose this was understandable considering I was staring down at my own lifeless body.

"Let's take a walk," he instructed.

He was a white dude, bald, sporting a well-cared-for goatee and wearing a navy-blue suit. By the looks of him, he had to have been in his mid-to-late thirties.

What the hell was he doing in our neighborhood? I wondered.

"But I can't just leave me here," I explained.

"That isn't you anymore," he said, with sympathetic eyes.

"Come," he continued, with a friendly nod. He extended his hand, and I took it without even thinking it over.

I tried everything I could think of to wake myself up as we walked. I even stomped my foot down on the pavement a few times – sort of like I did whenever it fell asleep. Nothing worked.

"You're not asleep, Angela," he interrupted. "You've passed on, honey."

I looked back when I heard screams coming from Kiki's front yard. They'd obviously found me. I wasn't really hurt that it took them so long to get out there. I mean, for all they knew, whoever aired her crib out was still waiting out there, nines drawn.

"Don't worry," he said, smiling. "None of them are coming with us."

"Who are you?" I asked boldly. I only considered it bold because he might have been God.

"I'm not Him, Angela," he said, grinning. You see, that also got me thinking he might have been someone like God or Jesus – his ability to hear my thoughts.

"My name is Michael. I'm an angel – the archangel to be exact."

I stopped walking. He didn't seem like anyone to be afraid of, but he wasn't exactly human, so I did grow a little nervous.

"Yours is a natural reaction," he admitted. "However, you've nothing to concern yourself with right now. I'm simply here to welcome you and inform you of your new position."

"Position?" I asked. I didn't see much point in keeping my thoughts to myself any longer.

"I'm an Angel of Death," he began. "And, you have been chosen to join me. Your role will be to help me and your fellow angels defeat the dragon, Satan, when the next great battle takes place."

"Satan?" I asked, even more overwhelmed than before – a feat I didn't think possible. "You want *me* to battle Satan? *Satan?* As in the devil? That Satan?"

He smiled. He did that often, it seemed.

"Like I said, you won't be alone."

"I don't know if I can do this," I said. "I mean…"

I glanced down at my body – at my small frame which seemed even smaller now. How could I possibly have been chosen for something like this?

He pointed to my heart. "This is all that matters anymore, child."

"Don't be afraid," he continued. "We've already defeated him once in the War in Heaven, and he was thrown down here by our Father. However, he was able to convince a third of the angels to side with him. He knows his time is short down here, so he's trying to build up his force of angels."

"For the next battle?" I asked.

9

He nodded.

I grew even more nervous.

"When is this going to happen?" I asked.

"It will take place at the end of time," he answered.

"Wait!" I blurted out. How far off was this? He said Satan knew his time was running out down here.

"It won't happen for some time," he said, attempting to calm me down. "Your mother won't live to experience it. She'll have been welcomed into the Kingdom of Heaven long before then. It's your friends I'm…"

"My mother!" I interrupted. I turned back toward the scene of my death. "I almost forgot about her! She doesn't even know! I need to go to her!"

He gripped my shoulder, and I glanced up into his eyes.

"You'll have your time with her. You'll visit her in a dream tonight to let her know you're okay. I'll see to it."

I suddenly recalled the night my grandmother passed away.

"Wait a minute," I began. "*Mi abuela* came to me in a dream the night she died. Are you saying that was really her? She really did that for me?"

He nodded.

"And I can do this for my mother?" I quickly added.

Again, he nodded.

"First, however, you need to know why *you* were chosen," he continued.

I have to be honest; even though this was miraculous, I was more focused upon my poor mother than what he had to say.

"I need your undivided attention, Angela," he cautioned. "I realize this isn't easy for you right now, but it is necessary."

"Okay," I said. "I'll try."

"The main reason you were chosen is to save your friends from heading down Satan's path, the wrong path. This will take some time."

I nodded, still a little unsure.

"And, as if this isn't enough, you will also be assisting me in collecting the souls of the deceased and carrying them to the Kingdom of Heaven."

"You want *me* to take lives?" I asked, concerned.

"I'm aware of what happened earlier, or rather what didn't happen," he said. "This will be different, Angela. It's something He expects of you now."

I wondered what the penalty was for saying "No."

I was already dead, so it wasn't like God could strike me down. And, not only was I a good Christian girl for the most part, but I was a good girl in general. I didn't drink, I didn't smoke, and I didn't sleep around.

I honestly thought I had nothing to worry about. I didn't think I needed to prove myself. Plus, I mean, God could handle this all without me. The first War in Heaven went well. No reason to think the next one wouldn't.

"You're afraid," Michael observed.

"Of course, I am," I admitted. "Who wouldn't be?"

"You're right," he said. "It's a normal reaction. Don't worry though. You'll have all the help you'll need. I promise. You'll never be placed in a circumstance you can't handle. God is putting you in this position because He knows you can handle it. Sound familiar?"

It did sound familiar. Probably because Mama would say the same thing anytime we found ourselves in a lousy situation (i.e. when my father left or when the electricity was shut off for a month). What a dirty trick?

Clearly, they'd been keeping tabs on me for a while - maybe even my entire life. Well, I suppose disagreeing with him would have been like poking holes in Mama's logic. I just couldn't do it. She was right every time. I think I even came out of all of those challenges a little stronger.

Maybe the same could be said for this challenge. I caved.

"Okay," I began. "I'm in."

"How am *I* gonna take lives though?" I asked, harkening back to my uneasiness around the gun.

"You'll simply kiss them and they'll pass on peacefully," he explained.

"The kiss of death?" I whispered, more to myself than him.

"Exactly."

"But can I ask you a question?" I said.

"You can ask me anything," he responded.

"I doubt this will work on Satan, so if I can't handle a weapon and I really can't fight too well, how does anyone expect me to hold my own in this great battle? It doesn't make any sense."

I really didn't want to do this. Why couldn't I have just died and that was it? On to the next.

"Remember what I told you about your heart," he suggested. "It's all that matters anymore. Just keep that in mind, and the rest will be there for you when you need it."

I didn't understand *how*. I mean, this was a pretty cryptic message, if you asked me. However, if a guy – or whatever he was – from the Kingdom of Heaven tells you not to worry about something, then I guess you shouldn't.

"I hope you're right," I said, and immediately wished I hadn't. "Of course you're right. I'm sorry. *Ay Dios mio.*"

I pressed my palm to my forehead. He laughed.

"*He* has faith in you, too," he explained. "Otherwise, I wouldn't be here right now. But *you* need to have faith in yourself; this is as important as anything else."

I seriously needed to get over this. I mean, for crying out loud, this dude probably spoke with God on the reg. So, if he told me He had faith in me, I'm guessing he wasn't just blowing smoke up my *culo*.

Ay Dios mio; I needed to clean up my language or, in this case, my thoughts.

I apologized.

12

"Apology accepted," he said. "It's understandable. You heard people speak like this every day, whether it was in person, on the television, or over the radio."

"Yeah," I agreed. "But now that I'm working for Him…"

"You've always been working for Him in a sense," he interrupted.

"Or, rather you've been *living* for Him, which is more important if you ask me. Too many people fail to realize this, or they just forget it. He should be shown the same amount of respect you show your mother, for you're His child, too. If there are certain things you wouldn't do or say in front of her, then you shouldn't do or say them at all because *He* sees and hears them."

He was right; he had to have been.

"I know," I agreed. "I'm sorry. It's just that my head is pretty much still spinning. First off, I was killed tonight – that alone was a lot to take in. Then, an *angel* paid me a visit. Not only that, but he wants my help fighting the devil. Plus, I mean, I still don't get how I'm all of a sudden gonna have mad fighting skills out of nowhere. It doesn't seem possible."

Without warning, he took a swing at me. Somehow, I just knew enough to sidestep his punch, grab hold of his arm – one hand on his forearm and the other on his bicep, bring it around his back into an arm bar, and guide him to the ground.

Ay Dios mio! I thought once again. Where did *that* come from?

"Convinced yet?" he asked, from his position, face down on the pavement.

"*Yeah*," I answered, flabbergasted. I quickly released him and helped him to his feet.

"See? As long as you have heart, and loyalty to the Lord, you'll be just fine. These are things Satan lacks."

He brought me to our house: ours – meaning my mother's and mine. Well, I suppose it wasn't mine any longer. She hadn't even gotten the call yet, the poor thing. I felt so bad for her, and there was nothing I could do.

13

She was just lying there, dead to the world; she must have been exhausted.

"I'll leave you to speak with her," he said.

I quickly turned to him.

"Wait!" I said. "You mean she can still see and hear me?"

"No," he answered. "The only people who will be able to do that from now on will be those whose souls you'll be taking. If they see you, they'll be dying."

"Then, how am I supposed to…"

"She's dreaming of you right now," he interrupted. "Anything you say to her, you'll be telling her in her dream."

"Really?" I asked.

"Yes," he said, and then stepped from the room.

I glanced back down at her and immediately began sobbing. Her eyebrows furled at just that instant; I must have been confusing her with my tears. I quickly fought through it and composed myself.

"Mama, I have something I need to tell you," I began.

Suddenly, the phone rang. I panicked as she began to stir.

"Mama! I'm okay! Just remember I'm okay! I love you! I love you!"

She rolled out of bed and walked by me on her way out of the room.

I didn't want to follow her out into the kitchen. I just didn't want to see her face when she received the news.

My grandmother's death had hit her pretty hard and she was *expecting* that. This was going to be far worse; her *beba* was gone. She'd immediately blame Lucia and the girls, and it technically wasn't *their* fault I was killed.

Even if this was an act of retaliation for something they'd done, there was no way they expected me to be at Kiki's crib that night.

They probably figured I wasn't even up for the first leg of my initiation. I didn't blame them, not even for a minute; I couldn't.

14

I chose to join them; they didn't recruit me. If I had just been me, then I might have survived that night.

Then again, God did have a plan for me, so I'm sure Michael would have taken me that night regardless. How else would he have done it, though? Car accident maybe? But I didn't even own one.

Actually, I suppose this cause of death made the most sense since I was chosen to save the Destinas.

"*Si*," Mama began, with the receiver pressed to her ear. "Sorry. Yes, this is she."

She shook her head. This was her routine whenever she mistakenly answered the phone in Spanish. Personally, I didn't think it was any reason to apologize. I never told her this, though.

"*Who is this?*" she shouted. "*You're lying! This is some sick joke! My daughter is not dead! You should be ashamed of...*"

She pulled the phone away from her ear. I could hear the dial tone. She was fuming. She didn't get this angry often, but a prank like this would have had anyone seeing red. Unfortunately, it wasn't a prank.

I wondered who the caller was. It had to have been one of the Destinas. Probably Lucia, if I had to guess. She liked Mama, and she definitely had our number. I get why she didn't give her name.

She probably didn't want to incriminate herself or wind up in a situation where she might have to snitch. She wouldn't have, and as a result, she probably would have found herself doing a bid for a crime she didn't commit.

Mama pulled her cellphone out of her purse and browsed her contacts for my number. She could have just checked her most recent calls, but she was old school. Hence the reason we still had a landline.

I wasn't looking forward to this call, because obviously, I wouldn't be answering. She still wouldn't believe I was dead, but she would be worried I was in trouble. Being out till all hours of the night in our neighborhood was a parent's nightmare.

15

Sadly, she'd be bypassing this nightmare only to find herself in an even worse one - grieving for her dead child.

Before she could end the call, there was a knock at the front door. In all of the excitement, I failed to notice the blue lights flashing out front. She failed to notice them, too.

Maybe it's because we were somewhat used to them by now.

Damn. This was it. They were about to confirm her worst fears. She'd know the caller was right - that it wasn't just some sick prank. Her world would crumble in an instant.

She took her time unlocking the door. There were two officers waiting for her when she finally opened it.

"Ma'am, is this the home of Angela…" the lead officer began to ask.

Trembling and teary-eyed, she cut him off.

"No! Not my Angela! It can't…"

She glanced back at the phone on the wall, then lowered her head.

The officer's eyes were filled with sorrow. Clearly, this was the part of the job he hated. You'd think he knew me personally and knew what a good kid I was, making this even more difficult. He didn't though.

As far as I know, he didn't even know I was friends with the Destinas. He was probably just heartbroken for Mama. Well, that and I was still pretty young. Another life cut short. He'd probably seen it often in his career - too many times to count. Not that he'd want to.

"I'm sorry, ma'am," he apologized. "I'm afraid Angela is dead."

She dropped to her knees. The thud reverberated across the room. She didn't faint. She was still conscious. Just sobbing uncontrollably. He knelt down to help her to her feet. His partner assisted. The lead officer then helped her to the sofa.

"I'm so sorry for your loss," he said. There really wasn't much more to say.

"Um, ma'am, we're going to need you to come downtown with us to identify the body," his partner said.

Guess I was wrong. There was more to say. *Ugh!* The thought of her having to identify my body hadn't even crossed my mind. This was going to be horrible. My mind jumped right to what I looked like when it first happened.

I really didn't want her to have to see it, but I guess she had to. I'm sure it's protocol.

She nodded, with tears still streaming down her cheeks.

The lead officer spoke up again. "We can leave whenever you're ready. Take all the time you need. We'll be waiting right out front."

The officers stepped outside and she dragged herself back into her bedroom, only pausing once to check in on mine. This, of course, only kept the tears flowing.

I looked to see if it had done anything to Michael, but he was emotionless – probably used to scenarios like this. Needless to say, I wasn't looking forward to my funeral.

"The choice of attending your funeral is entirely yours," he said.

"Not everyone is up for it."

A short time later, she was passing by us again, wearing jeans and a tee. I tried to follow her out the door, but Michael held me back. Evidently, he had more important plans for me.

"Sorry, Angela," he began. "I'm afraid you have work to do. There's going to be a car accident a few streets over in a few moments. You need to be there. You'll be taking one of the drivers involved. You know him; his name is Reynaldo Sanchez."

If he was the same Reynaldo Sanchez I was thinking of, then the neighborhood was going to lose two of us too soon that night. *Ay Dios mio.*

"Ahem, neither one of you will have been taken too soon," he interjected. "*You* were taken exactly when He wanted you. This will also be the case for Reynaldo."

"I know He has a plan," I said, frustrated. "What about our plans, though? Mine and Reynaldo's?"

He smirked, which of course annoyed me.

17

"It's never been *your* plan," he explained. "It's always been His."

"Well, why did He even give me a life, if He was planning on taking it so soon?" I asked. "Better yet, why did He do this to my mother? She didn't deserve this. She's a good woman, and certainly a good Christian; she gets to church every Sunday without fail."

His eyes were definitely sympathetic, I could tell.

"This isn't a punishment," he tried to explain.

I sighed.

"Look, I know this is frustrating for you, Angela," he said. "And I can understand your being angry with Him. You obviously love your mother very deeply and you're clearly protective of her. He gets that, *and* He appreciates it. However, He has greater plans for you than the both of you had. Trust me."

Thinking about Mama and how much I love her, it dawned on me that even in death, home was a safe haven for me. It was my comfort zone.

There were times when I was terrified to leave the house. I realize it makes me sound like some scared, little kid, but there was a dangerous world outside our doors. Look no further than what happened to me. I was an innocent…technically. I never officially joined the Destinas.

I didn't deserve any of this, but I was cursed with it, nonetheless.

There were days when I would literally run most of the way home from school. I could hear the other kids laughing as I ran by. If I had my way, I'd have never left that house - well, not as often as I did. They'd have all thought I was loco.

I was still scared of what was outside those doors waiting for me. It wasn't just the streets anymore. Now, I'd have Satan to worry about and whoever he had fighting alongside him. It dawned on me that I could stay in that house now if I wanted to, and no one would be the wiser.

There'd be no one making fun of me for it because no one would know about it. Also, I'd have all the time in the world with Mama. Good luck trying to talk me out of that.

"This won't feel like your house when she's gone, Angela," he explained. "Your mother won't live in it forever. Eventually, she'll be moving up there. We can use your help defending her forever home."

Damn. Well played.

"Now, come on," he ordered. "We need to get going. Reynaldo needs to be taken before his ambulance arrives. You're ready for this, right?"

"I guess I have to be," I said, somewhat childishly. "I mean, what choice do I have?"

I slunk my way past him –   more childish behavior exhibited. I'm pretty sure it was the same slink I went with whenever Mama sent me to my room. It's funny what you carried with you into the afterlife.

"You'll always be you," he said. "Remember, He loves you just as you are."

As upset as I was over everything, it was definitely comforting to hear him constantly refer to God in such a personal manner. I honestly couldn't wait to meet Him. I felt as though it would be very affirming for me.

While it's true I'd always been a believer, there were times when even I questioned His existence. For example, a lot of little kids have contracted cancer and died as a result of it. I've often wondered why He lets that happen. I mean, what good could possibly come of it?

I hoped Michael would shed some light on this, but he didn't. I guess even *he* couldn't comprehend every aspect of His plan. Perhaps we weren't supposed to. Perhaps He thinks we can't handle it. I don't know. Just a theory, I guess.

He smiled, accompanied by a nod.

Reynaldo already looked dead by the time we arrived there. By the looks of things, his Mustang had collided with a Ford pickup.

I wasn't sure who was at fault (not that it mattered), but both vehicles were on his side of the street, so it could have been on the other driver. Like I said, though, it really didn't matter who was responsible.

19

All that mattered now was I had a job to do. I needed to take Reynaldo with me.

He was still in his seat, with his head resting sideways sounding the horn. His eyes fluttered a little when I forced the driver's side door open. Luckily, he was the only one in there.

"There's no such thing as luck," Michael pointed out. His mind-reading was wearing me thin.

When it dawned on me that Reynaldo was still conscious, I glanced back at Michael, who was waiting patiently.

"He's still alive," I said. "Maybe he'll…"

He interrupted my thought process with a stern look. I should have expected as much.

I knew he was in pain and most likely wouldn't be walking away from this one, but I just couldn't bring myself to take him. There'd be no turning back after this. I'd never feel like me again; not the version of me I was comfortable with anyways.

I'd need to be a heck of a lot bolder now and maybe even a little less emotional. That wasn't me. I'm sorry. They had the wrong girl.

"There isn't much time, Angela," he said. "You're the one who has to do it."

As if on cue, a siren sounded a few streets away; the ambulance and perhaps a police cruiser or two were in route. I grew flustered and quickly leaned my head in, prepared to kiss Reynaldo on the cheek. His eyes stopped fluttering and remained open, staring directly into mine.

"Angela?" he asked, clearly confused.

I tucked a few strands of his blood-streaked hair back behind his ear. I was mothering him. He looked as though he needed it. We were never really all that close, but we were friendly with one another in passing and I believe we were in the same homeroom in either fourth or fifth grade.

I always thought he was kind of cute – very kissable, just a little shy.

Michael spoke up. "You shouldn't have any more earthly desires, Angela. And the only kissing I expect you to do from now on will be to serve a greater purpose."

"I'm sorry, Reynaldo," I apologized, just before I kissed him.

His eyes closed for good. I eased his head off the horn; I didn't want this to be the last sound he heard. It would have been a grim reminder of how he perished.

I may have been too late with this gesture, though. If I was to believe everything Michael told me, then sadly the horn must have been blaring when I ended his life.

He had already walked away, leaving me there to take it all in. I studied the scene intently before joining him. I was looking for the light people were always going on about or any other kind of sign indicating Reynaldo's ascension to Heaven.

"It doesn't look like anything out of the ordinary, Angela," Michael explained, without so much as glancing back at me. "Don't believe everything you've seen in movies or on television."

Shortly thereafter, I caught up with him.

"Now what?" I asked.

"*Now*, young lady, I want you to return to *su casa* and wait for *su Madre*," he said.

"*You* speak Spanish?" I asked, nearly as surprised as when he revealed to me he was an angel.

"Of course," he said, matter-of-factly. "I speak every language."

This blew my mind, but I suppose it made all of the sense in this world and the next. I mean, he was here for all of us, not just me and *my* people; we all had to go sometime.

I guess it just surprised me since he was a white dude.

"Why do you want me to wait for my mother?" I asked, reluctantly. I prayed she wouldn't be joining us anytime soon.

"It's nothing like that," he quickly explained, dismissing my concerns. "Though she won't realize it, you'll be a calming presence for her. And this will also be some much-needed closure for *you*."

"Thank you," I said.

He nodded. How did *he* understand? I wondered what he ever needed closure from.

"I'll have a new assignment for you following your funeral," he began. "It should be easier for you than tonight's was. You'll be taking the soul of an elderly gentleman who has led a long, oftentimes happy life. He's ready to come home. You'll be reuniting him with his wife and daughter. You'll find this is one of the perks of your new role."

I smiled. It felt like I hadn't done that in a while. He was right about my upcoming assignment; it was bound to be much easier on me than taking Reynaldo.

"It will be easier *on* you," he said. "But it won't be nearly as easy *for* you."

He had a serious look to him now. I was a little worried.

"Why?" I asked.

"Because he's at St. Joseph's Home for the Elderly. It's a nursing home, which means you're certain to find at least two of Satan's angels lurking about. For obvious reasons, they're drawn to nursing homes. Plus, they typically partner up. And they'll recognize you instantly. Don't be afraid, though. Simply remember that you possess what they don't; they lack what he lacks."

"Why do they typically partner up?" I asked. "What's that all about?"

"Because we're stronger than them."

And, just like that, he left me.

I was lying on my bed when I heard Mama's keys in the door. I missed my bed already and I hadn't really missed any time on it yet; that is to say I typically wouldn't have turned in for the night this early.

I'd also begun coming up with questions regarding my new way of life. For instance, would I be able to sleep anymore? Or, for that matter, would I even need to sleep anymore? I doubted it. I mean, I no longer had a body, so there wasn't anything to exhaust, right?

As annoying as it had gotten, believe it or not, I sort of missed Michael's mind reading.

I made my way out to greet her when I heard the door finally open. "Greet" might not have been the most appropriate word, but I suppose I was still greeting her with my "calming presence."

She was *done* – physically and emotionally drained by the looks of her. I could see it in her eyes and the way she gingerly meandered around. Poor thing.

Of course, she would have given me her patented *you know better than that* look if she'd ever heard me refer to her in this way. Humans weren't "poor things" in her opinion; this was a label you gave a *perro* that needed to be put down for some reason or other. Why, she'd even correct one of her girlfriends if she called one of the less fortunate neighborhood children a "poor thing."

But there she was, looking as poor a thing as anyone I'd ever seen.

She sat down at the kitchen table, and I did the same. Like it was any other night, she started in on the mail, thumbing her way through it. I could see she'd already done this earlier in the night, though, because a few of the envelopes had already been torn along the side; this must have been some sort of an attempt to take her mind off of what had happened.

Whatever worked, Mama. I took no offense.

She looked to the ceiling.

"*Ay Dios mio*," she said. "Please welcome her to your Kingdom of Heaven."

Por favor? Had I seriously left her with doubts? Aside from almost becoming a Destina, I'd led a fairly upstanding life if you ask me.

Nobody's perfect, but I like to think I was a pretty good kid. Still, I suppose it was kind of nice to find my mother still looking out for me; this was when you knew you had a good one.

This, of course, got me thinking about Heaven and my place in it. I mean, I obviously knew I'd made the cut. I simply wondered what it was going to be like. Was it *anything* like the movies depicted it? Was everyone hanging out on a bunch of clouds up there, or did it just look something like Earth without all of the garbage and bull… crap?

I caught myself as best I could even though Michael wasn't around; it was a work in progress. Speaking of him, I wondered where he was. Off recruiting another angel perhaps? I missed him. I suppose he was *my* calming presence.

I certainly could have used him alongside me over the next few days. These were days I should have been pleased with; family, friends and even neighbors I'd never seen before checked in on Mama and even brought her more dishes than our standard size fridge could hold. I wish I was able to fully appreciate all of this support for her.

However, I think it had finally sunk in for me. I was dead. I wasn't going to college anymore, I wasn't going to get married, and perhaps what hurt the most was I'd never have children, which also meant she'd never have grandchildren to dote on. Sadly, this was it for her.

"You get what you get, and you don't get upset, *mi hija*," was something she'd always remind me of whenever I felt cheated. I'm ashamed to say I dismissed these words more often than not. She'd be the first to tell you He doesn't owe us anything – that He'd already blessed us with more than enough.

As a child, this wasn't always the easiest thing to digest. Truth be told, even as an adult, it didn't go down so easy.

The end of each visit kind of sucked. At least, for me, it did. Most of *them* probably headed back home to their loved ones, while she was left with her memories and a ton of food she'd never be able to polish off on her own.

24

My Aunt Rosa handled the wake and funeral arrangements for us.

Emotionally, Mama was in no capacity to handle it on her own. She paid what she could and Rosa loaned her the rest. She could afford it, I guess; she lived in a huge house in the burbs. Well, it was huge to Mama and me.

The great thing about Rosa, though, was she never let any of this go to her head. She came back to see us all the time, and also invited us out to her house a lot. She even gave Mama a spare key to her house if you can believe it, for when they were out of town, I guess.

Mama refused it, though, in a polite way, of course. Maybe she didn't want to run the risk of losing it. Rosa's husband, Bob, was pretty cool, too. He was a middle-aged white dude, but he didn't act it. Sorry. I know that sounds bad, but I didn't mean it to.

They held my wake at Crowley Funeral Home, not too far from where we lived and even closer to where I died, ironically.

Every time I walked by it when there was a wake going on, I'd wonder who was in there. Not who was signing the guest book, but who they were there for. I could always tell when it was a kid because the street would be lined with cars, at least four cruisers would be parked out front in case anything popped-off, and the line of people would almost stretch to the end of the block if the kid was popular enough.

I never imagined I'd get this treatment, but I guess I underestimated myself. It seemed like *everybody* from the neighborhood was there to pay their respects and plenty more.

There were kids from school I'd never so much as spoken a word to. This wasn't because they were snobs or we had drama or anything like that; it was more because we had a huge school and I was for the most part a wallflower.

I certainly couldn't blame *them* for this; I'm glad they came.

Mama wore a black dress I'd never seen her in before. I guess it was her death dress. It looked a little snug on her, though, leading me to think she hadn't worn it in years and maybe that's why I hadn't seen it, or she borrowed it from someone for the occasion.

It's sort of strange referring to my own funeral as an "occasion," but that's basically what it was. Not all occasions are happy; there are plenty of solemn ones, too.

The Destinas showed up wearing white tees with my likeness printed upon them. I wondered where they got the picture because I'd never seen it before.

Printed beneath it in Old English font were the words "In Loving Memory," with the years of my life printed beneath them.

I don't know why I did the math; force of habit, I guess. Prior to all of this, I would have said there weren't enough years, but I had come to grips with the fact that this was what He intended, so it must have been the right amount.

"Atta girl," spoke a familiar voice over my shoulder, startling me.

I turned to find Michael standing there. He was glancing down at my body, running his hands along the casket.

"They did a good job with you," he admitted.

I tried to avoid looking at me lying in there as often as I could, but it's something you just *have* to look at; you can't help it. The flowers in my hair amused me. They weren't me.

"Yeah," I agreed. "Luckily, they…"

I caught myself.

"Fortunately?"

He nodded, so I continued. "Fortunately, they didn't get me in the face. Still, it might have been easier on Mama if it had been a closed casket."

We looked over at her. She wasn't standing to greet people any longer. The weight of it all must have finally forced her to sit in one of the comfy-looking chairs that lined the wall.

There were so many in that room, but she was the only one seated. Go figure. She was clutching the same tissue she'd been wiping her eyes and occasionally her nose with for the past hour or so. I looked around for a box of tissue; they always seemed to have one lying around at these places.

I eventually found one, but I guess it didn't really matter since I couldn't bring it over to her.

"So, who was it?" I asked Michael. "Do you know?"

"Does it matter?" he asked, smelling or pretending to smell some of the flowers I'd be buried with.

"No," I answered, only because I figured this was what he wanted to hear. "I was just curious, that's all."

"*You!*" Mama shouted, pointing her finger in Lucia's direction. She didn't look so weak anymore. "What are you girls doing here?"

"We've come to pay our respects," Lucia said.

She looked more sympathetic than anything else; you could tell she understood where Mama was coming from. Plus, it was probably no longer news to anyone that I was killed leaving a Destina meeting.

"We'll leave if that's what you want."

The rest of the girls nodded.

"That is what I want!" They were in the lobby already when she let them and everyone else in the place know that I didn't deserve this. *Gracias*, Mama.

I'd have to say the worst part of the entire experience for me came when the time arrived for them to close my casket before they brought me out and loaded me into the hearse.

This seemed to hit Mama the worst, too.

It must have been the finality of it all. It was closed; she'd only see my face in photographs from then on. She didn't drop to her knees or anything like that, but she *was* weeping uncontrollably. It looked like it was even affecting her breathing.

She didn't notice me standing there, though, so she must have been fine.

It was a little awkward in there to be honest with you. What I mean is the guys who were locking me in kept stealing glances at her; they could probably feel her eyes on them. It wasn't their fault, Mama. They were simply doing their job. There were probably times they hated their job. I bet this was one of them since I was only a kid.

My funeral Mass attracted fewer mourners than I'd expected. I figured everyone who showed up to pay their respects at the funeral home would have been at it as well. After all, I always felt as though the Mass was the easier of the two to attend – emotionally. I suppose it was the more difficult one, schedule-wise.

I didn't take offense. The entire Mass was spoken in Spanish. It sounded beautiful. Of course, it helped that Father Ruiz was far more eloquent than me. Mama always complimented him on his vocabulary; she considered him just about the most well-spoken man she'd ever known.

On this day, she was especially complimentary.

The cemetery side of it all was nice. I'd say they gave me a pretty good send-off. Most of the women and girls there took a flower from atop my casket and walked off with it; maybe it was something to remember me by.

I stood by Mama until it was just her, Aunt Rosa, and Uncle Bob. Everyone else had gone, even the priest. She still didn't see me. None of them did, which, of course, pleased me. It meant they weren't going anywhere any time soon.

"Ready for your next assignment?" Michael asked.

He didn't startle me this time around. I watched him descend. I waited for Mama and the others to head back to the cars before responding.

"I'm ready," I said.

"Now, remember what I said about who you'll probably encounter there."

I momentarily drew a blank. Then, it hit me. *How could I have forgotten about them?* Satan's angels.

"Right," he added, nodding.

Security was pretty tight at the nursing home; much tighter than I was expecting for a bunch of elderly people. You would figure they'd need hardly any security guards on site. And they say people don't respect their elders enough.

At least, *I've* been accused of this a few times. False accusations, if you ask me. Before she died, I'd sat through plenty of *mi abuela's* stories over and over. You have to really care about someone to suffer through all of that for them.

The place reeked. All I could smell when I first got there were soiled linens and whatever the hell else they stuffed into those plastic bins.

In practically every direction you looked you could see old folks roaming up and down the hallway. A few of them looked at me, but didn't say a word, so I couldn't tell whether or not they really saw me.

Each room had one or two index cards with the patient's info printed on it posted outside their doorway. A good amount of them also had a collage of their life hanging out there.

I wondered if these were the same collages you'd see while waiting in line to see them at the funeral home. Come to think of it, I didn't get the collage treatment. No biggie, though. This would have just been one more thing for Mama to struggle through.

Of the five people I found there who weren't in their "golden years," only two of them noticed me. They had to be the ones I was forewarned about.

They began approaching me, leaving the others behind at the nurses' station completely unaware. The one leading the way was sporting a wicked grin; actually, I suppose it was a devilish grin.

I was getting scared. Not gonna lie.

I know I took Michael down with ease, but he might have just gone along with it so I'd feel confident in my abilities.

These two weren't going to do the same. I needed to do this for the Lord, though. He wanted me to take that old man's soul, and these two weren't going to stop me.

The one out in front took a swing at me, but I was able to use his own momentum against him when I wrenched his arm forward, dropped down to the floor, wrapped my legs tight around his, and twisted us up, sending him face first into the wall. He slid down to his knees.

As quickly as I could, I drove him headfirst into the floor with everything I had. I was worried the carpet had softened the blow, but surprisingly, he stayed down. It was funny how throughout all of this commotion none of the staff heard a thing.

I was completely alone – not like they could have done much.

Suddenly, I was being thrown up against the wall.

It momentarily stunned me, dropping me to my knees. I was crouched over, gasping, when I noticed a boot coming up to my ribs. I was able to roll out of the way just before it got there.

I sprung up, spun the angel around and drove my foot into the crook behind his knee. Once he dropped to his knees, I wrapped my arm around his neck and locked it in tight. I squeezed with all I had until he stopped struggling.

For some reason, I gently lowered him to the floor instead of just letting him drop, and continued on to the old man's room. I discovered an eerie scene when I looked back over my shoulder.

The angels were sprawled out on the floor, while the nurses continued chatting away like nothing had happened.

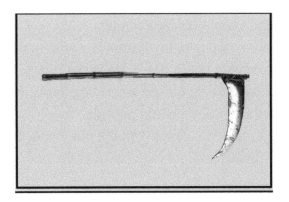

Chapter 2
Shawn

He didn't look good; that's all I remember about that day prior to Angela's involvement. I just sat there bedside, wondering if he was going to make it through the night and wondering why none of his surviving children, my mother's siblings, had returned any of my calls.

I guess I shouldn't have been too surprised. I mean, they really only cared about themselves; at least, this was my take on them.

He was in that nursing home for over a month, and two of his children – the ones who could boast they visited – only showed up once.

It was when he first got there, and I hadn't seen them since. In fact, the next time I saw any of them was at his funeral and then the reading of his will.

They weren't thrilled he left *me* the house – a house I'd lived in for three years, taking care of him.

When my parents were killed in a car accident my senior year, he had me come live with him. Even though his health was deteriorating, I held my own taking care of him for a while.

Once I began to struggle, he figured it was in our best interest to bring in the hospice nurse, Mary. She worked out nicely for a while, but when his condition took a turn for the worse, she broke it to me that he needed more assistance than we could provide.

She was right, too. He, along with the other patients at St. Joseph's, had a full team of support staff taking care of them, and believe me, they needed it.

Mary and I definitely would have been in over our head. They were great at what they did. In fact, the only time I ever feared for his safety was when I heard a commotion in the hallway outside his room one night.

I opened his door a crack and found a gangsta-looking girl attacking a couple of the people out there. That was Angela. Her victims didn't look like they were staff members, but this didn't matter to me.

I guess in all of the excitement it didn't even dawn on me that the actual staff members were ignoring these attacks. I doubt I would have tried to alert them to it anyways since I was so afraid; I wouldn't have wanted to draw her attention to our room.

I mean, in all honesty, if she manhandled those two guys who were considerably larger than me, then what was I going to do in the way of stopping her?

I really wanted no part of her. She was scary. I figured this was the last place I'd have to worry about a street thug, albeit a female thug. She certainly didn't fight like a female. Damn.

Not wanting to take any further chances of being discovered, I backed away from the door and sat bedside once again. I silently prayed she'd get what she came for and leave.

Suddenly, like I was stuck in some kind of a slasher flick, our door opened and she stepped in. I froze. *Pathetic.* She froze as well when she noticed me staring at her. She made it seem like *I* was the out-of-place one in that room. How's that for a twist?

Once she must have finally gotten over the shock of finding me there, she made her way over to the bed. I found the courage to stand up, but she calmly motioned for me to sit back down and I did.

She no longer seemed like a threat, and she was looking upon my grandfather with such caring eyes. Just as he looked up into those eyes, she leaned over and kissed him on the forehead. His eyes instantly closed and his breathing ceased.

He was *dead*.

She gave me one more confused look before she took off. I didn't know whether or not to go after her or stay with my grandfather. This whole thing was so outlandish I'd have been surprised if I *had* known how to react.

I mean, this girl had literally just given my grandfather the kiss of death after giving an all-out beat down to two full-grown men.

I'd like to say I stayed behind to protect him, but it was more an act of cowardice than anything else. Besides, the damage had obviously already been done; he was gone. Once I figured *she* was gone, I braved poking my head out into the hallway. Luckily, she was nowhere to be found.

"Hey!" I shouted toward the nurses' station, startling them.

"Yes?" a woman on the shorter side asked, incredulously.

I looked at her as though she had two heads. *Was she serious?* I thought.

"That girl just killed my grandfather!" I pointed toward the exit.

They looked confusedly at the door, and then back at me. Then, they all looked at me as though *I* were the one with two heads.

"What?" the nurse asked, dropping whatever she was doing or pretending to do. She then hurried over to me.

"What girl, honey? What are you talking about?"

She didn't even allow me to explain myself, rushing past me into the room. I guess she needed to confirm what I'd told her about my grandfather first. Made sense.

I let the door swing closed behind me. She was busy checking whatever needed checking. I'm sure there was a protocol to follow.

"Now, what's this about a girl?" she asked, without so much as looking up at me.

"The girl!" I answered, bewildered. "The one who just attacked those two guys out there."

I motioned toward the hallway. The nurse finally looked up at me, appearing utterly confused. Clearly, she hadn't seen a thing.

"What are you talking about?" she asked. "What attack?"

What happened? Was I losing it?

"In the hallway," I began. "She…"

"Dear, I think you may have dreamed all of this," the nurse suggested, which made more sense than I wanted it to.

"You've been spending *a lot* of time here lately, and I'm sure it's been exhausting at times. Couple that with a traumatic experience like this and it's completely understandable – your dreaming something like this."

"It was so real, though," I recalled.

"She looked right at me, and then kissed him on the forehead and that was it. He was gone."

The nurse sighed.

"I think it was a dream, honey," she reiterated.

I began shaking my head, but she cut me off, nodding.

"We were right out there the whole time. I didn't see anyone come into this room, and we all certainly would have noticed if some sort of an *attack* had gone on out there. Don't you think?"

"Yeah," I reluctantly agreed. "I guess you're right."

I glanced down at my grandfather's lifeless body. Unfortunately, the only part of this I knew for sure was real was that he was gone, taken peacefully in his sleep, and mine apparently.

34

"I'll notify his other surviving family members," she said.

"Thank you," was all I could get out before she left the room.

Unfortunately, I needed to rely upon my aunt and uncle to handle all of the funeral arrangements and whatnot; it was all a little over my head.

They came off like they were ready and waiting for it. I hated how they treated my grandfather with such disdain. My parents loved him. I don't know whether or not this sounds horrible – and I guess I frankly don't care – but I definitely think God should have taken one of them, or even both of them, and spared my parents.

Was it such a horrible thing to think, though?

The wake was as fake as could be. We all stood in line, with my Aunt Linda closest to the casket because she was the oldest and "closest" according to *her*; that was a laugh.

I wasn't even close to his casket, and I honestly felt as though *I* should have been standing where she was; it was a no brainer. Every now and then, she dabbed just below both eyes with a tissue. So badly I wanted to walk over and grab the tissue from her just to prove to everyone there that it was bone dry.

Her eyes weren't the slightest bit red and her cheeks weren't even close to glistening. I doubt she had anyone fooled.

At least my Uncle Peter wasn't even trying to fake his grief. In fact, there were times when he was actually laughing with the other "mourners," and they weren't even laughing over shared anecdotes of my grandfather's, which I guess I would have been fine with.

Even the condolences didn't seem all the way genuine. *Who were these people?* Four hours of this bull was about all I could stomach.

Luckily, the funeral itself was much shorter, and the only portion that really annoyed me was the eulogy. This wasn't because it was chock-full of lies slandering the poor guy or anything like that, though.

On the contrary, it's because it was pretty accurate through and through. The reason it pissed me off so much was that my uncle clearly knew his old man was a stand-up guy worthy of praise and he *still* treated him with such disdain at the end of his life and probably leading up to it.

To be honest with you, I wish he hadn't spoken at all; it would have seemed a lot more respectful.

I wanted to say something to him on the ride to the cemetery, however, my emotions had finally gotten the better of me, right there in the limo. I tried my best to hold back my tears, but I fell way short.

Aunt Linda, who was sitting beside me, placed her hand on my knee. To comfort me, I guess. It was working, too, until I snapped out of my crying fit and realized it was her. I quickly brushed her hand away.

The two of them were really messing with my mind and emotions that day. They were doing all of the right things, but none of it seemed right. What I mean is none of it seemed right for *them*.

I really wanted to say something to them, but nobody takes you seriously when you're struggling to reprimand them with the blubbering voice. It especially would have been ineffective on Uncle Peter; he might've even laughed at me.

Fortunately, I was with it enough to foresee something like this going on.

Peter wasn't a likeable guy at all. In fact, I'm willing to bet the only people who paid their respects to my grandfather in support of my uncle were his co-workers.

He didn't strike me as somebody who had more than a handful of friends at any given time.

His own son, my cousin Bryan, couldn't stand him. I never heard him come right out and say it, but I could just tell. Bryan's gay, and his father's one of the biggest, most vocal homophobes you'd ever meet. He was constantly bullying him over it.

Before he took a turn for the worse, my grandfather seemed to be the only one who ever got on my uncle's case about it.

What happened at the cemetery instantly made me forget about his stab at a eulogy and hers at motherly comforting.

She was there, dressed just as she was the night she took him from us. She wasn't hidden amongst the mourners like one might expect; instead, she stood right out in the open just beyond his gravesite for all to see – yet no one noticed.

She was pretty much staring me down throughout the goings on. Just as everyone was making their way back to their car, she walked off deeper into the cemetery.

I turned to my aunt and hugged her. She clearly wasn't expecting it. You can feel when somebody isn't expecting your hug; they almost always end it a little prematurely with the *okay, break it up* tap to your upper back.

I released her and discovered her bug-eyed expression awaiting me. My uncle just looked on, a little unsure.

"Just… thanks for what you did in the car," I said, and I suppose I meant it, too.

"Oh… okay," she said, then offered my uncle a bewildered glance.

"I think I'm just going to take a walk to clear my head," I explained.

"Um, okay, dear," she said, before checking her watch.

"Just don't be too late, okay? We're having everyone back to my house."

"Oh, you can go ahead," I suggested. "I've got my phone on me. I'll call for a ride when I'm finished. This could take a while."

She looked a little unsure.

"Let him go, Linda," Uncle Peter said.

"He'll be fine, and I need to pick up some beer on the way."

Why was I standing around as though I needed *their* permission? I slowly turned and walked off in Angela's direction, not even sticking around for Aunt Linda's approval.

Angela must have known I'd come after her; I knew a slowed walk when I saw one. She was reading somebody's stone when I finally caught up to her.

"Is she one of yours, too?" I built up the nerve to ask.

She turned to me.

"What?" she asked.

"Her," I said, motioning to the headstone of a woman who'd died a year and some change earlier at seventy-five.

"Did you kiss her, too?"

"*No*," she said, looking offended I'd asked.

Had she forgotten she was the reason I was there? It wasn't such a far-fetched notion she'd kissed this woman, too. I mean, something had to have drawn her to this particular stone.

"Well, yeah, a lot of times; just not in the way you mean. She was my grandmother."

"Oh," I began. "Sorry."

She went back to staring at her grandmother's stone.

"What are you, by the way?" I asked.

She seemed to go on the defensive when I asked this.

She looked like your typical young woman. I think the only thing that stood out for me was that she could easily hold her own against two full-grown men.

Also, I'd have been willing to bet my inheritance most people couldn't kill a man with a kiss. Combine all of this with the fact that apparently only *I* could see and speak with her and my question seemed a lot more reasonable than she had given it credit for.

She still didn't have an answer for me and we were probably nearing the minute mark, so I pressed her.

"A ghost?"

She seemed to be, at least, entertaining this one.

"Are you really?"

"Not exactly," she finally said. "At least, I don't think so."

"You don't *think* so?" I continued. "So, then, you might be? I only ask because it seems like I'm the only one who can see you, and I'd hate it if that meant I was crazy."

She smirked.

"You're not *loco*," she explained.

I only knew about a D's worth of high-school Spanish (if that), but "loco" was pretty much one of the words everyone knew, thanks in large part to pop culture. At least, I'm willing to bet this was why I knew it, so, thank you, Cypress Hill.

"I'm an angel," she revealed. "My name's Angela."

"I'm Shawn," I said, as though I were chatting it up with a regular girl.

For some reason, an angel wasn't quite as frightening as a ghost. Still, I thought angels were supposed to be peaceful and, you know, winged.

What she did in that hallway was anything *but* peaceful, and, aside from the obvious differences, the make-up of her body didn't seem all that different from mine.

"First of all, I was defending myself," she began. "Secondly, I haven't earned them yet. And, oh yeah, I can read minds now, too."

I'm afraid I had nothing for her at that point, be it verbally or mentally. Exactly how do you follow something like that?

"I was checking on *you* today," she added.

"*Me*?" I asked, incredulously. I shrugged my shoulders. "I'm fine, I guess, other than the fact that I have no idea what's going on right now."

She looked like she had something important to tell me, but she decided to keep it to herself, whatever it was. This wasn't very fair considering she could read minds and I couldn't. Now, she looked a little disappointed.

"You're right," she said. This was going to take some getting used to – her hearing my thoughts.

"Okay, I think you're hot," I blurted out. "At first, I'll admit I was a little turned off by the whole gangsta girl thing, but I'm over it. And I figured I might as well just tell you now, so I don't make things awkward without realizing I've made them awkward."

She smiled, blushing.

"Thanks, but my days of earthly desires are behind me," she gently replied.

"Hmm, well, that's definitely the kindest way I've ever been shot down," I admitted. "It's much easier to swallow than the old *I just want to be friends*. And apparently this is one of those cases where it really is you, not me. So, thank you for that, I guess."

She laughed.

"Is there some place we can talk in private, so nobody thinks you're losing your mind?"

"Sure," I answered, looking around. Personally, I didn't really care what any gravediggers thought of me. Anyone I needed to worry about had already gone back to my aunt's house, I assumed. "We can walk to my place. It isn't too far from here."

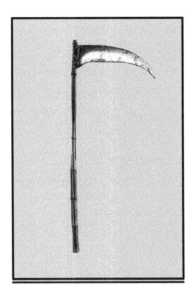

Chapter 3
Angela

He didn't seem sick. If he was terminally ill, he certainly didn't act it. *So, why could he see me?* It didn't make any sense. Then, it dawned on me. His plan wouldn't always make sense to me.

Once I'd accepted my confusion, I found I had a new concern: whether or not to tell him he was so close to death. *Ugh! Why did I feel the need to check in on him?* I had enough on my plate with saving the Destinas.

Still, I guess this would have been as good as any other time to take him. I could tell right away how lost he was when we got back to his place; he was very alone.

"He's left you with a huge void, hasn't He?" I asked.

"Yeah," he answered, matter-of-factly. "But it's nothing I'm not used to by now. My parents died a few years ago, so I've gotten to be pretty good at handling loss."

"Well…" I began to say, still searching for the right words.

"It's not a quality I've found comforting," he interrupted. "It's better than *not* being able to cope with it, though."

He sighed.

"The thing I hated the most was…"

He paused for a moment. He was afraid to share something with me.

"Just say it," I suggested. "I'm going to find out regardless. I have my ways. Remember?"

I winked at him, hoping to lighten the mood.

"Right," he said, with a smirk.

"Here goes. The thing I hated the most was their wake. It's something I'd never wish on my worst enemy. Both of them were waked at the same time, which I guess made sense. They were in separate rooms, though, so I needed to keep walking back and forth every so often.

"The lowlight of the evening was any time somebody would tell me they were in a 'better place now' and that God must have had plans for them. Correct me if I'm wrong, but hadn't He already given them a plan? Weren't they down here to raise me?"

He awaited my response. I didn't have one for him; I was still fairly new to this myself.

He continued. "This time around, the 'better place' bull was much easier to stomach."

"It isn't bull, Shawn," I explained. "I know you don't want to hear it, but your parents *are* in a better place."

He chuckled under his breath and looked away.

"Well, I suppose I can take *your* word for it," he said. "At least you've been there."

"Briefly," I said, smiling. "Just after I took your…" My smile faded.

"What's it like?"

"I really can't explain it. I couldn't see any of my loved ones, but I certainly felt them. That was enough for me."

He was disappointed.

"Faith has never been about what you can see, Shawn," I explained. "It's always been something you feel. Otherwise, we'd have all seen Him or, at the very least evidence of Him, a long time ago."

"I like that," he began. "In fact, I'm going to use it."

I smirked.

"Do me a favor. Only use it if you feel it."

He nodded.

"Hey, what was it like on your way up there?" he asked.

I didn't answer him right away, so his mind naturally started to drift to what *he* figured it was like.

He pictured a transparent version of my body sort of rising out of my actual body and just continuing on up through the clouds and whatnot.

Then, he pictured like a huge gate waiting there for me – which I'll admit would have been cool, but he couldn't really picture how high up beyond the clouds I'd have to go to get there because, I mean, he'd been in airplanes that had risen over the clouds before and obviously there was nothing heavenly at that altitude; nothing he could see, at least.

I started to chuckle and quickly covered my mouth.

"I think you've seen too many movies," I said.

"More like cartoons, I think," he corrected, slightly embarrassed.

"Well, I doubt either medium has it right," I replied.

He paused for a moment to build up what he deemed some much-needed courage.

"Okay," he began. "Then, what *is* it like? You still haven't answered my question. Or is this one of those meaning-of-life type questions you're not supposed to answer for anyone?"

"I wanted to mess with you a little and make up something *completely* ludicrous like… some mad long escalator made of gold stretched down from the clouds, and I stepped on and rode it up to the gates. Ironically, I think I might have seen something like that in a cartoon once.

 This definitely would have been funny, especially if you bought it, but it doesn't matter because I can't lie anymore. I can't commit any sins anymore actually, which is obviously a good thing. Don't get me wrong. I'm not complaining."

"That would have been good," he said. "I'm not sure I would have believed you, but you never know."

"I sincerely hope you wouldn't have believed me," I said, smirking. "The truth is I didn't *see* anything, but I definitely *felt* a lot."

At first, he seemed kind of bored, as bizarre as that may sound. He wanted to hear about some cool visuals.

"Sorry to disappoint you," I apologized. "It was all feeling, no seeing."

His eyes widened; he was mortified. I think he kept forgetting I could hear his thoughts.

"Actually, *I'm* sorry," he came back with. "It appears I need to be a little more mature about this. What kinds of things did you *feel*?"

"I wasn't aware of it at the time, but I ended up feeling the guilt of all of my sins at once," I began.

"Honestly, at first, it just felt kind of weird – an uncomfortable sort of weird. Once I was told what it was I was feeling, though, it all made sense to me. I could remember pretty clearly how I felt back when I had first committed a lot of these sins – how guilty and even nervous I felt.

"It all raced back to me in one fell swoop. Then, when it was finally over, I felt better than I'd *ever* felt. Let's just say it was a very ethereal feeling."

He nodded, but he had no idea what ethereal meant.. He'd heard it often enough, but he never got around to looking it up. Chalk it up to laziness; his opinion, not mine.

"Heavenly," I said, with a smile. "Simply put, it means heavenly, and that's exactly how it felt. Heavenly. I could tell I was there."

The more he thought about it, this *was* awesome, and he thought it made perfect sense.

The thing he liked most about it was that you couldn't convey something like this in a movie. He was glad I shared it with him. And it did get him thinking about all of the sins he'd committed, which then got him thinking about Jesus taking one for the team. He figured Jesus probably felt everyone's sins, and that it must have damn near broke His heart.

"*Probably*," I quickly agreed.

He seemed to be getting it. What a relief. Now, I just needed to get him to be more at peace with the loss of his parents, which I didn't expect to be easy by any stretch.

"How familiar are you with the Bible?" I asked. "Specifically, the Old Testament?"

"Not as familiar as I should be," he admitted, slightly embarrassed.

"I could never get past all of that begetting business in the beginning. I don't know if I have undiagnosed ADD or what, but they lost me pretty quickly once they got going on that. I read the first five or so lines of it because I felt I owed it to Him, but I gave up shortly after that."

I understood where he was coming from. It was awfully redundant, but it must have been noteworthy.

"Well, if you *had* stuck it out, you would have read about the Israelites – His 'chosen people.' They were pretty selfish for the most part; they were kind of the *Now Generation* long before that phrase was coined. They wanted everything He had planned to bless them with pretty much right away. They didn't feel like they should have had to wait around for it. They didn't get that to receive His blessing they first needed to live according to His plan.

"The reason I'm telling you this is because you need to know that your parents *have* received His blessing. They've endured His plan and now they truly are in a better place. It isn't always easy, but it's always worth it."

"Yeah, but hearing it from *you* is one thing," he began. "Hearing it from them, though…"

"It shouldn't matter where you hear the truth," I said. "All that really matters is that it's the truth. Right?"

He nodded again.

"People still don't want to hear that in certain circumstances, though," he said. "At least, I didn't want to hear it, not after my parents had just died. You know?"

I nodded this time. I started thinking about all of the mourners who had said the same about me to Mama. It was probably ten times worse for her to have to hear it. I mean, until I discovered the bigger picture, I was with everyone else in thinking no mother should have to bury her child.

"How did your parents handle it?" he asked, as though *he'd* read *my* mind for a change.

"*My parents?*" I asked. "Um, it was just me and my mother. Dad took off shortly after I came into the picture."

"That sucks," he said. "I'm sorry."

"Don't be. We were fine up until I died."

"How did it happen, if you don't mind my asking?"

I grinned and shook my head. Talk about a question I thought I'd never be asked.

"Gunned down," I said. "Drive-by."

He knew it, or so he thought.

"I wasn't in a gang, Shawn."

"*Oh*," he began, with sympathy in his eyes. "Innocent bystander?"

"Well, yes and no," I said. "I wasn't in a gang, but this was only because I chickened out of my initiation. I was leaving my girl's crib when they aired it out."

"Aired it out?"

"Shot it up," I tried again. "Is that better?"

"Sorry," he apologized. "I suffer from a mild case of suburban whiteness."

I laughed, though this did get me back to wondering *why* he could see me. Again, he looked pretty healthy.

"So, how are you feeling?" I asked. "I mean, aside from all of this."

"I'm fine. Why?"

"Just curious."

I almost broke the news to him, but I chickened out at the last minute. This seemed to be my MO as of late. I also avoided discussing Mama's handling of my death. It was a little too soon for me, and I felt as though I needed to remain undaunted around him.

"So, do you hate the people who killed you?" he asked.

Almost instinctively, I shook my head. He was in disbelief.

"You don't?"

"No. I mean, how could I? After all, they didn't target me. If it was who I think it was, they probably didn't even know who I was. Besides, He wanted me there."

"Hmm," he began. "I guess you're right. You can't really be angry with them if it was out of their control."

"Now, this isn't necessarily an excuse for any other wicked thoughts they might have had over time," I cautioned. "Sometimes, Satan's at work."

His eyes instantly widened at mere mention of this name. He started nervously pacing around his living room, peering out through the front windows from time to time. Eventually, he found his way to the sofa and began rubbing his palms up and down his thighs to calm himself.

"So, he is real?"

"Yup," I confirmed, perhaps a little too matter-of-factly for him. "He's down here."

"Whoa!" he exclaimed, quickly rising to his feet. "I thought he was down *there*."

He pointed to the floor.

"So did I," I admitted. "But I've since been told otherwise by a very reputable source."

He gulped.

"I'm sure you have."

He looked as though it was the end of the world already; he was silently conceding defeat.

"Don't worry, Shawn," I said. "He's outnumbered."

He was relieved for the time being.

"But, he is trying to build his forces up," I cautioned. "It's on me to help prevent this, specifically in the case of the Destinas – my girls."

"Is that the gang you were trying to join when you got...?"

I nodded. He clearly didn't feel comfortable discussing death with me, at least my own.

"Yes," I answered. "And I'm afraid they're headed down the wrong path. It's up to me to save them."

"How?" he asked. "Not to dampen your spirits, but aren't gang members pretty much set in their ways?"

"They are, and the Destinas are no exception. So, I need to convince them that He's waiting for *them* to change because *He* never changes. They need to understand that they can't continue doing things the way they're doing them if they want His blessing.

"When their time of judgment comes, they can't just cut a deal with Him like so many others have tried to do. You see, typically, a person's greatest desire for change is born of desperation, not obedience. It's on me to get this message across to them."

He was once again relieved.

"Well, that should be easy enough to do," he said.

"Just pay them a visit. Even the toughest, most loyal gang member would at least hear you out. I mean, for crying out loud, you're going to be visiting them from beyond the grave. I'm guessing they'll believe just about anything you have to say.

"And they were obviously fond of you, so they'll no doubt take it to heart. *I* have, and we'd never even met before all of this. *They* know you and they also know for a fact you died."

"This is true," I began. "But the only problem is they can't see me. Otherwise, I most likely would have scared the *caca* out of them when they showed up at my wake."

He was suddenly creeped-out, even more so than before.

"Your *wake*?" he asked. "What was that like?"

"Strange," I admitted. "Very strange, in fact. I spent a lot of time looking at myself, needless to say."

"I'll bet," he sighed. "Did they do a good job or were you all fake looking?"

"They did a pretty good job," I had to admit. "It's probably easier appearance-wise when it's a younger person. Wouldn't you think?"

He nodded.

"Did they do a good…?" I started to ask, but quickly caught myself.

"Closed casket," he answered. He knew where I was headed.

"Sorry," I apologized. This apology could have been for a couple of things.

"No worries," he said, smiling. He changed the subject. "Why couldn't *they* see you?"

Oh no. I preferred our other topic of discussion – the less uncomfortable one. My days of sinning were behind me, so I unfortunately had no choice but to level with him.

"They couldn't see me because they apparently aren't dying any time soon."

His expression, as expected, turned grave.

"Wait. People can only see you if they're on their way out?"

This was just what I was hoping to avoid. Well, I guess it was inevitable. He'd need to find out sooner or later. At least, this way, he'd have time to prepare for it. You know, come to grips with it so to speak.

I nodded. I felt terrible delivering this blow.

"How long do I have?" he asked, with a brave face now. "Do you know?"

I shook my head.

"And, no, I don't know how, either," I added.

He sighed.

"I want to help you," he said.

Help *me*?

"Okay, you've piqued my curiosity," I began. "How are you going to help me?"

His second guessing gave him away. He didn't say a word, but he'd clearly forgotten about my newly acquired talent.

"You're going to stick out like a sore thumb in my neighborhood," I said. "You know that, right?"

He nodded solemnly.

"They probably won't take too kindly to you."

This didn't sway him any. I was impressed.

"I've already been given a death sentence anyways, right?" he asked.

"It's better if you don't look at it that way," I said. "He's calling you home, Shawn."

He rolled his eyes. I didn't get on his case about this even though I probably should have. Michael would have.

"You're right. I'm sorry. I guess I'm just an angst-monger."

"No," I disagreed. "I don't think that's the case. I think it takes years to earn a label like that. You're just a little pissed off, and rightly so. Believe me, if I could have, I'd have withheld this news a little longer. That was the silver lining in my death: I had no idea it was coming. Sorry."

He shrugged his shoulders.

"Hey, it is what it is."

Surprisingly, he wasn't pretending to be brave. This wasn't a brave face he'd put on; this was *his* face.

"I'll be your messenger," he announced.

"You're sure about this?" I asked, offering him a chance to rethink things.

I braced myself for any kind of a reaction from Michael; none came.

"Yeah," he confirmed. "I mean, if I don't have much time left, then I might as well make what time I do have count. Don't you agree?"

I nodded. He was right. I think I would have done the same if given the opportunity.

He showed me around the house. It was nice, much nicer than ours. His grandfather must have done well for himself.

"So, who gets the house?" I asked. "You?"

He chuckled. "That would be nice. We find out tomorrow. His attorney's going to read his will."

I picked up a framed photograph of his grandfather from the bookshelf. He looked a lot healthier than the man I kissed a few days earlier.

"Hey, you don't already know whether or not I'm getting it, do you?" he asked.

"Sorry," I answered, sort of embarrassed. "I only read minds. Fortune-telling isn't in my repertoire."

"I just figured with all of your *His plan* talk, you might know something."

I shook my head.

"Well, I'm glad you only stressed the words '*His plan*,'" I said. "Had you accompanied them with air quotations, we might have had drama. Ya feel me?"

He shielded himself with his hands.

"Okay, okay," he joked. "I don't need any after-life drama. I'm here to help, remember?"

I hugged him. I'm not entirely sure why; it just seemed like the moment called for it. There was nothing more to it than that, I assure you.

"What was that for?" he asked once I had released him.

"You're making a major sacrifice for me," I explained. "I just thought I'd show my appreciation."

"Thanks. But, how much of a sacrifice is it *really*? I mean, I'm dying anyways, remember?"

"This is true, but most people would probably opt to spend their remaining time more selfishly. Maybe they'd go on a vacation or throw a huge party for themselves or find some other way to spend all of their money.

"You, on the other hand, have decided to help me take on Satan. It doesn't get much more selfless than that."

He was blushing now.

"Thanks," he said, followed by a sort of nervous laugh. "Still, I'm not sure I agree with you that those other people are being selfish doing any of those other things. For all I know, I'd have done the same if it weren't for you."

"Actually, you probably wouldn't even have known your days were numbered," I reasoned. "Again, I'm sorry."

"Don't be. We all have to go sometime. I'll get to go out something of a hero, I guess."

"There's no guessing involved," I said. "You'll definitely be regarded as a hero."

Even though he'd already volunteered, I felt as though I still needed to sell him on it. He'd given me a sort of concerned look when I mentioned taking on Satan.

We eventually ended up at one of the upstairs bedrooms. He turned to me, confused.

"Do you sleep?" he asked.

"I haven't yet," I answered. "But thank you just the same."

He smiled and nodded. I found him very hospitable. I suppose a few years of taking care of another person does that to you.

When dinner time arrived, he opted to order out even though he had become a "pretty good cook" over the past few years. With all that had gone on, he'd neglected his grocery shopping; this was certainly understandable. It sucks he hadn't received the same attention from his neighbors that Mama had from ours.

He checked his wallet. Apparently there wasn't too much in there. He felt awkward over what he was about to ask.

"Can you even eat anymore?"

"Possibly," I answered. "I don't know. Why?"

I smirked. I knew why.

"Because I'm going to order a pizza, and I need to know whether or not a small will cut it."

"Go for it," I said. "Even if I can eat, I hardly ever eat more than two slices – three, tops."

He sighed. He thought I was just being nice.

"Look, am I bothering you with my stupid questions?"

"They're not stupid," I said. "Half of the time, I wonder about the same things. I've even wondered if I'd need to use the bathroom anymore."

He stared at me blankly. He was embarrassed to ask, but he needed to know now that I'd brought it up.

I shook my head. He nodded as though my question had been a no-brainer. He was a funny one.

I couldn't taste the pizza, which was unfortunate because it looked delicious. I guess it made sense for me not to be able to taste it considering my taste buds were buried with the rest of me. I ate three slices anyways, so he wouldn't feel bad.

I stared at the ceiling in his guest room that night. His grandfather's bed looked more comfortable, but he wasn't ready to let anyone sleep in it just yet, not even an angel. I couldn't blame him. He wasn't rude about it, and, besides, I wasn't even sure I *could* sleep. This was something else I hadn't done in days, and I wasn't feeling it so I guess I didn't need it any longer.

He lost a lot of sleep that night, too. His mind was on the following day's meeting with his aunt, his uncle, and his grandfather's lawyer. He wondered whether or not he'd need to find a new place to live and whether or not he could afford it if he did. Sadly, there wasn't much I could do to help him there.

I let him go there on his own. He wanted some space for this, but he didn't feel comfortable asking.

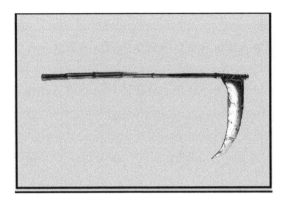

Chapter 4
Shawn

I was exhausted the following morning. I'm pretty sure I saw every hour on the clock throughout the night. Between the reading of the will and my angelic houseguest, I had a lot on my mind.

And, oh yeah, let's not forget I was apparently *dying* as well. I thought I was going to cry myself to sleep, but it never happened. You'd think I would have since I teared up a little over my grandfather's death; this should have easily been more damaging. I mean, who are you closer to than yourself?

While my life wasn't the best (far from it, in fact), I still wanted it to last for as long as possible.

We sat in Mr. Alexander's office, waiting for him to finish up with something. He had a stack of what I assumed was unfinished work resting on the far corner of his enormous oak desk. I doubt he could have even reached it from where he sat. That desk and that stack proved to us just how successful his practice was. Good for him, I guess.

I glanced over at my aunt and uncle. They were both sporting grins that would have annoyed me to no end if I wasn't dying. I had faith they'd eventually change their ways. I guess I just wanted to be around to see it firsthand. They'd seek forgiveness at some point; I was sure of it.

I was just praying it'd take place long before they were on *their* death bed. It would have been nice if they had done it while I was on mine; it would have been a decent going away present.

Still, I felt like I owed them something. I felt like I needed to forgive them for everything before I left, so I could pass on with a clear conscience. I figured the Lord would expect nothing less of me.

Since Mr. Alexander was still keeping us waiting, I stole this opportunity to let them know they were forgiven – that we were good.

"Aunt Linda? Uncle Peter?" I said, leaning forward in my chair and glancing over at them.

"I just want to say that I'm fine with the way you two have been the past few years. None of this could have been easy for you, and I guess we all deal with these things differently, right? While I wouldn't necessarily have acted like you did, I need to realize we can't all be held to the same standard."

I finished with a thumbs-up for some reason and eased back into my chair. He looked insulted and she bewildered, which, in hindsight, I suppose made sense. I know I wouldn't have liked hearing it even if it *was* the truth.

Suddenly, Uncle Peter thought I was up to something. He lurched toward me, leaning right over her, and let me have it.

"Listen! I see what you're trying to do here," he began. "You're trying to make the two of us look bad in front of him."

I began to shake my head, as did Aunt Linda, but her shake was far more subtle than mine.

He continued. "Well, guess what? It won't work because everything's already been divvied up, sport, it's been decided who gets what. All he's doing is *reading* the will. He can't change a damn thing in it."

"That's not what this is about, Uncle Peter!" I exclaimed, definitely hurt. "Honestly, I don't care if I get anything."

"*Yeah right*," he said, rolling his eyes. "This is really low, you know that?"

I shrugged my shoulders and followed with an exasperated head shake; I had tried. Oh, well. He wasn't the one I was concerned with pleasing anyways. Neither was she, but I shot her a glance just to gauge her reaction. She didn't seem to be siding with him. She looked more confused than anything.

"You really don't care whether or not you get anything?" she asked, probably just to make sure I understood what I was saying.

"No," I said.

Mr. Alexander momentarily lifted his focus from whatever he was finishing up with to look at us with furled eyebrows. What was he so ruffled about? He was getting his money regardless. Uncle Peter noticed his sudden change in demeanor.

"None of that matters," he said, rather smugly. "You're gonna get what you get. I'm not paying him extra to draw up more legal papers for us."

Apparently, this was the end of it, at least for the time being. Once he heard I'd be inheriting the house, though, he was all up in arms.

"What? This is *ridiculous*!" he exclaimed. "He wasn't even the man's child. He was his grandchild for Christ's sake!"

He was certainly doing a lot of pleading. This was when my mischievous side reared its ugly head; bad Shawn!

"Oh, um, all *he's* doing is reading the will," I reminded him. "He can't really change anything in it."

Aunt Linda wanted to laugh, I could tell. She did still waver back and forth between amusement and disappointment, though.

While I'm sure it still stung that I'd gotten the house, she didn't seem as beat up over it as him. Perhaps she wasn't as much of a pain in the neck as I'd originally thought.

In fact, I even wondered whether or not I should have gone ahead and written out my own will just to make sure the house went to her next. She was definitely the lesser of two evils.

By the time I left the lawyer's office, I started to grow agitated with the fact that I was dying; talk about an inconvenience. I really wished I'd never met Angela. This was when I began toying with the idea of ditching her.

I went out with the logic that she couldn't kill me if she couldn't kiss me. It made sense, right? I knew I had just inherited a house and abandoning it would easily be the most difficult choice of my life, but the keyword here was "life." Hell, I'd live in my car if it meant I was living.

While it's true I promised to help her out with her friends, this was when I had figured I was destined to die. When I took this detail out of the equation, I needed to go back on my promise.

I took a left out of the parking lot, heading farther away from my neighborhood. I hoped she wasn't hip to what I was doing. I really had no idea what she was capable of; I didn't know much about angels when it came to all of that. Until I met her, they were pretty much mythical to me.

I mean, I knew they were in the Bible, but I figured *I'd* never have anything to do with any of them. They were one of the things the God-fearing side of me believed in but the rest of me wasn't quite sold on. It's difficult to explain.

It didn't take me long to reach the conclusion, though, that if I were going to believe any of it (the Bible, I mean), I guess I needed to believe all of it.

I started thinking about going to church with my folks, a chain with the cross on it my godfather gave me for my First Communion, and even Christmas.

None of these things had ever scared me before. Now, all they did was remind me I was going to die. Then, I pictured the New Jersey Devils' logo, which I'd never given much thought to before because the devil always seemed pretty mythical as well.

Suddenly, he was as real as anything, and Angela needed my help to take him on.

I guess I was part of all of this now, whether I liked it or not. Once I finally came to grips with this, I pulled into the next parking lot and turned around. Maybe she knew this was all going on in my head and she sort of just let it ride its course.

"I tried to leave," I confessed, upon entering my house, which was apparently only a loaner.

She sighed.

"I sort of anticipated you'd second guess yourself at some point," she said. "You did volunteer your services pretty hastily, after all."

I nodded.

"So, what made you come back?" she asked.

It wasn't anything I *wanted* to do. I figured I was in too deep by that point to do otherwise, or so I thought.

She cast me a slightly disappointed look.

"*Well*, I am, aren't I?" I asked. "I have to die now. It's not like you're going to let me out of this."

It wasn't my intention to plead, but this was clearly the result.

"I don't know how to convince you this isn't a punishment, Shawn," she said, with sorrowful eyes. "He's calling you home."

"Then why did He even bother giving me this life?" I asked, pretty agitated by now. "I mean, I don't get it."

"And you're not supposed to," she explained, practically reprimanding me. "I don't get it either, and I didn't get why He took me at such a young age. What I do get, though, is that this is the way things need to play out.

"A lot may or may not be riding on your involvement. *I'm* willing to bet it is. Otherwise, why else would you have seen me when I visited your grandfather the other night?"

"I'm sorry," I apologized. She obviously had no say in anything she did or needed to do going forward. "It's just that this is all so…"

I shook my head, unable to finish my thought.

"Crazy," she replied. "I know. I'll do whatever I can to make it less crazy for you. I promise."

There was a sparkle in her eye; how fitting for an angel.

She was beautiful. I wish she wasn't. Every now and then, I caught myself staring at her eyes and then her lips – a habit of mine.

Even though I knew very well what her lips could do to me – what they were called upon to do to me – I continuously found myself longing for them. Just a little taste was all I needed.

What the heck was wrong with me? They were hazardous yet luscious; deadly yet heavenly.

I was all jammed up.

"They're off limits, Shawn," she said, just before curling her upper lip.

"Sorry," I apologized. "I guess I'm pretty weak. Pathetic, really. I mean, here you have these lips that are fatal – capable of a kiss I won't walk away from – and I'm infatuated with them. Thank God one of us no longer has any earthly desires."

"I'll keep you in check," she said. "Don't worry."

She winked afterward. Initially, I took it for flirting, but it obviously wasn't. I wanted it to be. I guess this was part of my problem. Maybe I shouldn't have turned around; I'd have probably been better off just about anywhere else.

"*Don't worry,*" she repeated.

"You're right," I said, and then tried clearing my head of any immoral thoughts since immorality was a sin and I really needed to worry about that kind of thing now.

Actually, I suppose I always needed to worry about it. It's just that I always thought I had plenty of time to repent for it; not the case anymore.

"Okay," I continued. "So, what's the plan?"

She looked reluctant to share whatever she had with me. Either she barely had anything yet and it was still a work in progress, or she simply wasn't confident what she had in mind would work.

"Well, I tried to summon Michael for his input," she began. "But…"

"Michael?" I asked, hoping I wasn't out of line.

"The archangel," she answered. "It takes some getting used to. I know."

I nodded. I found myself nodding a lot. When it came to circumstances like this, you really needed to let others steer you through it.

"Am I going to be meeting any of these people or beings or whatever I'm supposed to call them?" I asked. I wasn't being selfish. I sort of just wanted to experience it even if it was only briefly.

"I really couldn't say," she said. "I certainly hope so."

I caught myself staring at her again. This time, however, it wasn't in a lustful manner, not even remotely. I think I was finally beginning to picture her as one of them. She was no longer of this world, which meant she was unattainable. I needed to remain in this mindset. If she'd sprouted wings, it definitely would have been helpful. She laughed.

"Okay," I blurted out. "So, again, what's the plan?"

"Right. For starters, where do you keep your Bible?" she asked.

I suddenly grew embarrassed. I felt horrible. Never thought I would feel guilty about not owning my own Bible; I honestly never thought I'd be called out on it.

"*You don't have a Bible?*" she asked, incredulously.

"I've never had…" I mistakenly began.

"Don't even say you've never had 'the need for one,'" she interrupted.

"No!" I quickly responded. "I was going to say that I've never had it in my head to pick my own copy up. I just assumed there'd always be one around if I needed... it."

I sighed. She was right, and we both knew it.

"It isn't a chore, Shawn," she said. "You should want to read it. Everyone should, even if it's just for a little while, here and there. You should look at it as a handbook for life. It's God's word, after all."

"*I know*," I said, exasperated. I think I was more annoyed with myself at this point. "It's just that…"

She arched her eyebrows.

"It's just that what?" she asked. She was sporting a *this ought to be good* expression.

"I've always figured that since I knew right from wrong and pretty much followed the main rules to a T, I'd have been fine going forward. I'm sure I'm not the only one who does this."

"I doubt He only wants us to follow the main ones, Shawn. I'm pretty sure we have to try to follow all of them."

She shook her head.

"Let's go shopping," she said.

If you ask me, she was kind of forcing it. I mean, I wasn't totally oblivious to Biblical wisdom. I did pick up some scripture along the way. The old man saw to that. He didn't force feed it to me either.

What he did was have me bring him to church every Sunday. He couldn't get there on his own or so he claimed, so I had to bring him.

At first, I asked him if I could wait in the car; and, I did the first few times, but then I started to feel a little guilty about staying out there - especially whenever I saw him walking alone and gingerly across the church parking lot. It wasn't long before I was accompanying him inside on a regular basis.

I'll be honest. The more I went, the more rejuvenated I felt. I mean, I wasn't unhappy with who I was prior to that. I just felt like I was doing something to perhaps better myself now - sort of like when you start exercising more often.

That was my go-to New Year's resolution every year. To its credit, attending church with the old man ended up having more staying power than exercising regularly.

It was awkward holding the door to the bookstore open for her when most, if not all, of the people there couldn't see who I was holding it for. I received a few looks, but this was something I'd need to get used to.

We headed directly for the Religion section. I'm not sure why, but I felt uncomfortable with all of the other religions being showcased right there alongside the Bible.

I know how haughty this sounds, but I didn't mean it this way. I definitely respected the various religions out there, even though there were some I didn't necessarily agree with on some issues.

"Different people have their own ways of worshipping Him, Shawn," she said.

"The important thing to remember is that they *are* worshipping Him. Most religions share His message; it's just that there have often been followers who have unfortunately misinterpreted this message. It's probably happened in every religion, even Christianity."

I guess she was right, and she certainly said it tactfully.

I pulled one of the smaller Bibles from the shelf and instinctively checked the back for a price. She gave me a look. They wanted $14.95 for it. I thought this was ridiculous considering it was the word of God.

It should have been free for crying out loud, kind of like the Yellow Pages. I mean, honestly, what gave somebody the right to turn a profit with the Bible?

"Maybe the churches profit from it," she suggested.

"I don't see how," I said, ever the pessimist. "I mean, for starters, how would they even divvy it up when there are so many different denominations out there? Who gets to decide?"

She shrugged her shoulders, with her eyebrows arched. My expression must have shown my disappointment with her response.

"You know, I don't all of a sudden know *everything*," she explained, somewhat condescendingly. "Only God does."

She was right, and besides, why was I getting so bent out of shape over it? Either way, somebody was getting my fifteen bucks.

"Well, you can't take it with you anyways," she reminded me, trying to comfort me, I think.

That was one way to comfort somebody – remind them they're dying in the not-so-distant future.

"You're right," she said, along with something bordering on a smirk. "I'm sorry."

I skimmed through what would be my first and last copy of the Good Book. I'm not ashamed to admit I went with the New International Version because it was easier to read. Bring on the begats.

She laughed.

"Aw, we'll go through it together," she joked, mussing my hair some.

"There are a few specific passages I have in mind for dealing with the Destinas."

A salesgirl, probably in her early- to mid-twenties, approached us; she caught me completely off-guard. She was only mildly attractive, standing there beside Angela.

On her own, her rating would have been a bit higher.

"Can I help you?" she asked. "I noticed you talking to yourself while you were scanning the shelves. This is typically a dead giveaway that you can use some assistance – and perhaps some other type of help."

For the moment, I thought she was the crazy one; it was easy to forget just how invisible Angela was sometimes. This was one of them, especially considering I had just been comparing them side by side.

Marie – I checked her name tag in the meantime – began to look a little more attractive. I remembered she was the attainable one here.

"You can't do that to her," Angela pointed out. "Think about it."

Do what to her? Oh, right. Since I didn't know how much time I had left, I probably shouldn't have been courting anyone. Was this what she was getting at, or was she growing a little jealous?

"That is *so* not the case," she said; she was adamant about it, too. "I just don't think it would be fair to her. *That's all.*"

Marie craned her neck to see which book I was holding. She gently gripped my wrist and turned it to get a better look at the cover of my book.

This was definitely flirting – I don't care what anyone says. It just figured I'd been in and out of that bookstore plenty of times over the years and not once had anyone flirted with me, but now that I was dying, I probably could have left there with a phone number and perhaps even a coffee date.

"Sorry," Angela apologized. She meant it, too, I could tell.

"The Bible, huh?" Marie asked.

She scoffed, which spoiled the mood some.

"Yeah," I answered. "Why?"

"No reason," she said, nonchalantly. "I'm just not that into religion."

"Oh?"

"I could take it or leave it," she continued. "I'm just not sure how much of it I buy. I mean, especially with that."

She motioned to my Bible, which I gently tucked under my arm as though I were protecting it. These days, I felt like I owed it to it.

Angela wasn't pleased with Marie; she was as close to furious as an angel could probably get. I hoped she didn't think Marie was undoing everything she'd done. I deserved a little more credit than that.

65

"You should ask to see a manager," Angela suggested, but I didn't deem this step necessary. After all, everyone's entitled to his or her opinion. I shook my head; Marie thought it was at her.

Even though I wanted to see where this was headed, I thanked Marie and strode off toward the cash register. The girl who rang me up asked me if I wanted to become a member of some club to receive ten percent off of this purchase and any future ones.

I laughed, which, in hindsight, was pretty obnoxious of me. Damn morbid inside joke.

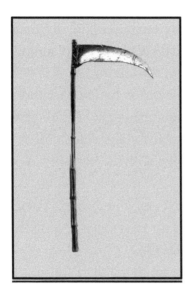

Chapter 5
Angela

That night, we really hammered out a plan and hoped it jibed with God's. Oddly enough, though, the more foolproof we made it, the more nervous Shawn grew.

It should have been the other way around. I held off on calling him on it because I wanted him to come around on his own. I was confident because I kept thinking back to what Michael had said about my heart.

I'd heard it said once by somebody other than him that "the Lord looks at the heart." I was banking on it. Perhaps this was what Michael was referring to. I figured Shawn's heart would be just as valuable as mine, if not more so.

Just from what I'd already witnessed, I could tell his heart was in the right place; I just needed to make sure it remained there. He doubted himself from time to time throughout the planning process.

I was doing most of the talking; he was doing the reluctant nodding. Life had really done a number on him so far, poor thing.

"Hey, you're going to be great," I said, gripping his hand. "I wouldn't be giving you such a major role in all of this if I didn't think you could handle it. It's just like with the hardships you've faced so far in your life.

"God wouldn't have put you through all of that if He didn't think you could handle it. He'll never set any of us up for something we can't handle. It's just the way He is."

This only comforted him a little. I fell short; he wasn't quite there yet.

"I don't get why He needs *me* for this," he complained. "I mean, He's God for crying out loud. He can beat the devil no problem. Right?"

"He is going to beat him," I confirmed. "Using us."

I was hoping he'd consider this an honor; *I* did. Yeah, it was scary and definitely overwhelming, but it was also something we got to do for Him. As far as I was concerned, it was a huge deal.

"I guess I just feel like such a long shot going into this," he said.

"They – whoever they are – are probably going to have a field day with me. I mean, I don't even make eye contact with shady-looking characters out of fear that I might accidentally start something with them, and now I need to deliberately start something with *Satan*?

"This is crazy, totally out of character for me."

"I'd say you're more like a dark horse than a long shot," I pointed out, hopeful. "Think about it. They don't know anything about you. You're our secret weapon."

He looked at me incredulously.

"I know, I know," I began.

"But you need to remember that when He's for you, nothing can beat you. It all comes down to two things: your heart and your loyalty to Him.

"Michael told me this when he first persuaded me to join the fight. He says these are things Satan lacks, and they're the things that will lead to his downfall again. Hey, it worked the first time, right?"

"So, he sold you on it, and now you're doing the same to me?"

"It's more than just talk, Shawn. Yeah, I didn't believe it at first either, but then I beat up two pretty big guys with ease, and it wasn't like they couldn't fight. So, you tell me."

He had somehow forgotten about this. I don't know how; it *was* pretty impressive.

He rolled his eyes and briefly chuckled. He couldn't believe this was happening to *him*, of all people.

"*For* you, Shawn," I corrected.

"Right." He nodded.

"David was a long shot, too, you know," I said, hoping to motivate him some. He didn't know who I was talking about, though.

"David from the Bible?"

He was growing frustrated with my name-dropping.

"Listen," he began. "I know you mean well with all of this, so I hate to break it to you, but I don't really know too many people in the Bible. I'm sure I've heard a lot of their names over the years, but other than the major players, I don't really know a thing about most of them."

"Yeah, well, David did play a pretty big role," I explained. Man, you would have thought I personally knew David.

He shook his head. "Sorry."

"I appreciate your honesty," I continued. "I'm talking about the David who defeated Goliath."

His face suddenly lit up.

"Oh, okay!" he exclaimed. "Davey and Goliath."

I shook my head, chuckling under my breath.

"No, no. Not the Claymation show about the boy and his dog. I'm talking about the real…"

"Yeah!" he interrupted. "The kid with the slingshot who took out the giant, right?"

I nodded. There was hope yet.

"Like I said, he was a long shot – a big time long shot, in fact – when he decided to go up against Goliath," I began.

"What happened was Goliath was talking trash about God and people were getting sick of it. None of them would do anything about it, though, on account of how much bigger he was than everyone else.

"But, then David comes along and catches wind of it. Like everyone else there, he's kind of pissed off with Goliath disrespecting the Lord like that. He decides he's going to do something about it, but Goliath doesn't take him seriously since he's even smaller than most of the cowards there.

"Anyways, one thing leads to another and David pulls out his slingshot and grabs a rock."

I suddenly slapped myself in the forehead, startling him.

"And, bam! That's all she wrote. He felled the giant, lopped his head off, and went on to become king."

"A slingshot, huh?" he asked.

"Yeah," I answered. "But I don't think it was the slingshot that killed Goliath. I like to think it was David's heart and his loyalty to God that did the trick."

Shawn smirked.

"What?" I asked, feigning innocence.

"Nice try," he said, grinning. "I see what you're doing. And it's working."

Overcome with joy, I bear-hugged him.

"Okay, now you can really hit me with the plan," he said.

I proceeded to lay it out for him. I went a little fast at first, mostly due to my eagerness; he needed me to slow down.

I composed myself and rewound for him. "The first thing you'll need to do is gain the Destinas' trust."

He looked very uncomfortable.

"How do I go about doing that?" he asked. "I'm a white dude from the burbs and they're a Mexi…"

"Puerto Rican!" I corrected, raising my voice a little. We weren't Mexican; we were Puerto Rican. There wasn't anything wrong with being Mexican; *we* just weren't Mexican.

"Okay," he slowly said. "So, how am I going to gain their trust?"

"The girls will definitely think you're *loco* when you first approach them," I said. "Once they know you're with me, though…"

"Um, their *dead amiga*?" he asked, trying not to sound too condescending.

"Oh… yeah… that's right." Talk about a monkey wrench.

He nodded; he felt bad for me. Reality can even sting an angel, I guess.

"You'll need to hit them with a few memories only they and I would know about," I continued. "My initiation! Nobody else was with us for that, so they'd have to believe you. I mean, it wouldn't make any sense for you to know the details of my initiation without having spoken with me. Right?"

"True," he admitted. "But what happens if I scare the you-know-what out of them and they decide to shoot me over it?"

"They shouldn't do that," I said. I was going to joke with him that they'd probably only knife him, but I decided not to go there.

"*Shouldn't*? So, you're not entirely sure? Well, that's just great."

"I want you to read about Samuel tonight," I said. "His story will be particularly helpful in dealing with the Destinas."

He nodded, and began thumbing through the pages of his Bible.

"You'll find him in the Books of Samuel. Pay particularly close attention to his interactions with God regarding King Saul. Read through Book 1 chapters 13-15 a few times. You should try your best to memorize them because if people see you carrying a Bible around our neighborhood, they're liable to take you for a Jehovah's Witness, and they don't fare so well."

He grew anxious.

"Do you think I'll get beat up or anything like that?" he asked.

I quickly shook my head, trying to calm him down some. I think I shook it too fast for that, though.

"No," I said, matter-of-factly. "It's nothing like that. They'd never beat up a man of God or what-have-you, they just won't open their doors for you, and we need the Destinas to open theirs for this to work."

"Okay," he said, reluctantly.

Again, he began thumbing his way through his Bible. I noticed he was in the New Testament.

"Um, you'll want to be in the Old Testament for this one," I pointed out.

"Oh, right," he said, skimming back. "I forgot."

I chuckled.

"You didn't forget. It's more like you never knew."

I embarrassed him.

"Busted," he grumbled. "You know, if this angel thing doesn't work out for you, you'd make one hell of an interrogator."

I arched my eyebrows and crossed my arms.

"*Heck* of an interrogator," he went with this time around.

 "I mean one heck of an interrogator."

"Much better," I said, grinning. "You're definitely a work in progress. Now, get reading."

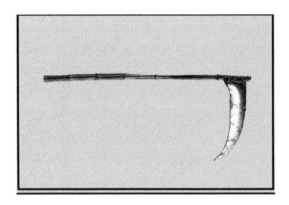

Chapter 6
Shawn

Not that she was the boss of me or anything, but I got going on Samuel right when I turned in for the night. I read through the chapters she mentioned a few times without any problems; this new, easier-to-read Bible was something else.

Every other one I'd ever read from prior to this reminded me a lot of Shakespeare in that I'd get the general gist of what was going on, but I wasn't all the way there. With Shakespeare, it was no big deal. However, with the Bible, you didn't really want to miss anything.

Anyways, this new version was a huge help.

Pretty much right away, I got why she wanted me to read those specific chapters. It was on him to deliver the bad news to King Saul that he was no longer going to be king; God himself had decided this.

Samuel needed to let Saul know he was on the wrong path and that he needed to change his ways. Nobody likes to hear that, and nobody likes to be the messenger in a scenario like this. Samuel, within reason, was worried Saul was going to have him killed; I would have been, too. I mean, this was probably where they got the expression, "Don't kill the messenger."

Oh, man! That's when it hit me; I was going to be a similar messenger, and I was even doing it on God's behalf in a roundabout way.

I started to connect with Samuel really quickly. In fact, in a panic, I jumped ahead to see how he made out. Luckily, he was fine. Even when he eventually died, that didn't last long; he came back to life a little later. I think I nodded off at this point.

Somehow, I doubted things would run this smoothly with the Destinas.

My worrying not only cost me some sleep that night, it also hurt my chances of memorizing what I needed to. I got the gist of it, though; this was good enough, as far as I was concerned – it needed to be. I think it would have been better coming from me anyways – in my own words, I mean.

It might not have sounded as genuine if I had simply quoted Scripture to these female thugs.

I later discovered they're called *thug misses*, not *thugettes*; luckily, I didn't end up using this for an ice-breaker because it might have gotten me killed even sooner.

I tried to treat the following morning like any other, but I struggled with this approach. I kept thinking it could easily be my last.

"They probably won't kill you," Angela said. "Believe me. They're not like that. Not all gang members are heartless killers. More often than not, they only kill for a reason and I doubt you'll be giving them a good enough one."

"See? There's that uncertainty again. I wish you would just…"

"I know," she sighed.

"I wish I could tell you you'll be perfectly safe today, but I don't know for sure and I no longer have the ability to lie – not even what I once considered a harmless, white lie."

Whenever I started to see her as a regular person, she always seemed to remind me of her nagging, heavenly restraints.

I had a difficult time picturing what life would be like without the ability to sin. Yikes! What does that say about me?

She brought me to Kiki's house, which I guess was the go-to Destina hang-out. It was where the second stage of her initiation took place and where she met Michael.

She showed mild trepidation when we first got there, but I guess this was normal since the last time she was there she died a violent death. I wondered if she had any flashbacks going on.

"It's not that," she said, now anxiously scanning the yard.

"Then what is it?" I asked. "What's got you so worked up?"

"I have the feeling I'm not the only angel here."

I myself began scanning the yard. At the time, she was the only one I could see.

"You won't be able to see him until I get into it with him," she explained.

"That was the only reason you could see the other two."

Just as she was finishing her thought, she was knocked to the ground from behind. I quickly grew a pair and spun to face her attacker; there was nobody there.

I backed away from where I stood, completely freaked out. This was pointless, though, since I couldn't see him anyways.

It was easily the most frightened I'd ever been; she was still down and I had no idea how to prepare for what I figured was coming.

Luckily, I didn't need to concern myself with this for long. He appeared when she tripped him up. I could tell she wasn't at a hundred percent just yet, and he still had enough of an upper hand to wrench her to her feet by the hair.

Something drove me to intervene when I normally wouldn't have, but she quickly brushed me off as she struggled to maintain her balance. Clearly, this wasn't my fight.

Fine by me, I thought. I got to just hang back and watch her do her thing again.

She took him out with a move that looked straight out of a mixed martial arts training manual.

It started out as this sort of arm bar thing that didn't look like much at first, but once she wrenched back on his arms, I could hear at least one of them break followed by him wailing in pain.

She left him sitting there for a moment, screaming with both arms limp at his side. Honestly, it was a little difficult to watch.

I thought he'd had enough, but she clearly wasn't on the same page, because she kicked him directly in the chest, forcing him onto his back. She immediately mounted him, though this probably wasn't a necessary measure.

A few days earlier, I'm sure this would have turned me on. Then again, she was a different person when she was fighting – kind of scary, actually.

"*Who are you here for?*" she screamed.

Spit flew from her mouth she was so pissed off. He tried to squirm out from beneath her, but I think he would have needed his arms to make any real headway.

"*Which one of the girls?*"

She must have realized he wouldn't be sharing anything valuable with her because she lifted his head from the ground, and with a sudden twist, broke his neck. My jaw hit the ground just as his head did.

She confusedly scanned the yard over and over again from atop her victim. Once she was finished, she glanced over at me.

"We need to get in there to see what's going on," she said rather calmly, as though she hadn't just taken a life.

I turned toward the house, which now had a very ominous look to it. It didn't really. I mean, there wasn't any noticeable difference in its appearance from that of the other houses on the street. It was just that I didn't need to face a fear of mine in any of the others.

On top of that, I got back on the whole impending-death thing I needed to get used to so I wouldn't spend my remaining days stressed out.

People always go on about how there's always somebody out there going through the same thing as you, facing the same struggles. Somehow, I doubted this logic applied to me this time around. I was pretty sure this bad boy was all mine.

"As far as I know," Angela chimed in.

"Man!" I began. "Can't I have even a minute to myself?"

She chuckled, rising to her feet.

"Sorry," she said. "Unfortunately, I can't really turn it off. It's just one of those things."

I shook my head, somewhat frustrated. I knew she wasn't necessarily going to be criticizing my thoughts or anything like that, but still, there are some things you just want to keep to yourself.

"They're still being listened to, you know," she said. "By Him."

"Yeah, I get that, but at least He never comments on them."

"*No*, but He does act on them. And He always has your back. This is something I want you to consider going into this, okay?"

I nodded. You can't really reason with somebody who's been through what she'd been through. She'd been amongst the all-knowing; I'd only been amongst the wild guessers.

"Maybe we oughta call Michael in on this one," I suggested. "Just to make sure the you-know-what doesn't hit the fan and I end up dead."

She snickered, or at least, I took it for a snicker.

"You want the *Archangel of Death* here to make sure you don't die?"

I guess it did sound a little ridiculous. I just figured that since I was now such an integral part of this plan, he'd want to keep me around for a while.

"Who says you're integral?" she asked.

"Oh, I just sort of assumed I…"

"Relax," she said, grinning. "I'm just messing with you. Honestly, I have no idea what's going to happen in there, but I do know we wouldn't be in this position if we couldn't handle it. And Michael would be here already if he needed to be.

"I know you can't hear my thoughts, so I'll share my dominant one with you. I'm wondering when and how you're going to die. It's been at the forefront of both our thoughts for days."

I simply stared at her for a moment. I was jealous of her position for a number of reasons.

First and foremost, whatever was waiting inside for us really couldn't hurt her physically. Emotionally, she'd probably be somewhat vulnerable – depending on how close she was to these girls.

Secondly, she no longer had to concern herself with when, where, and how she was going to die – actually, I suppose she never needed to worry about these details. Her death had to have been a complete shock to her – a legit Pearl Harbor job.

I bet she was a goner before she even hit the ground; at least I hope she was.

"I think I was," she said. "Michael was there. He probably knows for sure."

"What's he like?" I asked, stalling, but still genuinely curious.

"He's kind of a pain in the neck," she admitted. "For the first few days, he was all about the pop-in visit. And, yeah, I'll admit the mind reading took some time to get used to. It's mad annoying. Believe me, I sympathize."

"It must be kind of cool, though, to have that ability."

78

"Yes and no," she replied. "It is kind of cool to know I can't be lied to, but at the same time, I feel a little guilty that you no longer have any thoughts to yourself when you're around me. Plus, it isn't easy to hear a person pity himself and then desperately plead with God to spare him."

I lowered my head. She gently gripped my shoulder, prompting me to look her straight in the eyes. They were a gorgeous shade of brown – almost tan – and definitely warm.

"You have nothing to be ashamed of," she explained. "I think it would be stranger if you didn't beg Him to let you live."

I hugged her; it felt called for.

"Wish me luck," I suggested.

"There's no such thing," she was quick to point out.

"Do it anyways," I added.

She rolled her eyes.

"Good luck."

I climbed the front steps. My shoes felt weighted. I immediately rang the doorbell and glanced back at her. She looked almost as anxious as I felt.

I heard feet hurrying to the door and over to the windows. It should have occurred to me that it really wasn't a good idea to startle a group of likely armed gang members who had recently been the intended target of a drive-by that had resulted in their friend's death.

Really, though, unannounced was the only way I could visit, so it wasn't actually a poor choice on my part.

The front door opened, but the screen door – which was thicker than any I'd ever seen – remained shut for the time being. A somewhat overweight Latina peered out at me. She didn't say a word; she simply stared.

"Who is it, Kiki?" another girl asked from behind her. I craned my neck to see who was speaking. She responded by giving me a better look at her gun.

"I don't know," Kiki replied. "Some *white boy*."

She seemed more confused than upset with me.

"Can I help you?" she finally asked.

This wasn't the response I was prepared for at all. I figured I was going to have one or two expletives thrown my way. Instead, she probably greeted me the way her mother taught her to greet visitors years earlier.

The gangsta visage temporarily took a backseat to that of the polite hostess' daughter.

"Oh, um, I'm not really sure how to say this, but…"

She covered her mouth and suddenly swung the door open to step to me. I instinctively stepped back and nearly toppled down the front steps.

"What is it?" she asked. "Is it my mother? Did you find her?"

Two of her friends made their way to the doorway once she asked this. Now, I obviously didn't know her, or any of them, from a hole in the wall, but I felt like I was seeing a side of them a lot of people didn't get to see.

"No!" I answered. "I'm a friend of… Angela's."

"You mean you *were* a friend of Angela's," said the first girl to step in between Kiki and myself. She must have been Lucia, their leader. Angela had briefed me on her.

"*Actually*," I began, followed with a deep breath. "I am her friend. In fact, she's here with me, now."

Perhaps I should have eased into this because I suddenly had a gun pointed at my face; it belonged to Lucia.

"Normally, I feel bad for somebody who's a little *loco*," she said. "But you're bringing my girl into this. That's disrespectful. And coming around here, spitting that stuff, is just foolish."

I grew even more nervous. I glanced back at Angela; Lucia noticed this and naturally took a look for herself, now aiming her gun at Kiki's front lawn instead of my face. Her confusion told me she wasn't a goner anytime soon, or at least she wouldn't be leaving by way of Angela.

"Give them some things about me only they and I would know," Angela quickly suggested.

"Like what?" I asked, with probably a little too much attitude. In all fairness, though, we hadn't gone over any of this. I was equipped with zero Angela anecdotes.

"Who are you talkin' to?" Lucia demanded. Again, she poked her head out, gun drawn.

"Angela," I said, matter-of-factly.

"Oh, tell them I couldn't shoot Lil' Marie!" Angela shouted. "And... and that the nine had blanks in it."

"Nine?" I asked, feeling pretty out of the loop.

Lucia quickly brought her gun back up to my face. I reached for the sky as though I was being held up.

"Who has a nine?" she shouted. "You?"

"No," I answered, with my arms still above my head. "What the hell is a *nine*?"

"It's a gun, Shawn," Angela explained. "Tell them the gun I was supposed to shoot Lil' Marie with had blanks in it."

"Angela says the gun or nine or whatever you call it that she was supposed to shoot Lil' Marie with had blanks in it," I said, hoping this would do the trick.

Lucia lowered her gun, bug-eyed, so it must have.

She grabbed me by the shoulder and hauled me inside. Before she shut the door, she gave one last look outside. I'll bet she was even more on edge than usual because of what had recently gone down out there. Like I said, I didn't know her from a hole in the wall, but she seemed pretty alert for *anyone*.

The door was eventually shut, leaving Angela out there. Lucia bolted it. This worried me since the night she paid my grandfather a visit, Angela needed to open the door to his room to do so. Damn! I was on my own, or so I thought.

A hand poked through the front door, made an unusual gesture and then disappeared from where it came. None of them seemed to notice. My guess was Angela had learned a new trick. Seconds later, all of her stepped through the door. She was beaming; I smiled.

She stood off to the side as they formed a semi-circle around me. As unsure as they seemed about me, I sort of felt like I wasn't human – like I was some sort of an alien species. Granted, I *had* just told them I was hanging out with their deceased friend, and then pretty much provided them with what I hoped was irrefutable evidence.

"Alright, which one of you knows this crazy white boy?" Lucia asked, looking around suspiciously. It was like she had let this little charade of ours go on for long enough. Naturally, every one of them was as bewildered as the next. "For real?"

"None of them," I reluctantly broke in. I was afraid of her, no doubt about it. Honestly, I think she would have been intimidating even if she hadn't stuck a gun in my face. I could tell they all felt the same; it was on their faces – especially right then.

"I'm telling you the God's honest truth," I added.

"*How*?" she asked. "How can my girl Angela, whose wake we *all* attended, be here with you right now? It's impossible. You're crazy."

I sighed, fully realizing she wouldn't believe what I was about to share; none of them would.

"She's an angel," I announced, looking at her first and then at the rest of the girls. My eyes eventually made their way to Angela herself. They must have been focused on her longer than I thought, for a few of the girls – Lucia included – soon joined me in looking over there. The girl closest to Angela stepped away from her – just in case, I guess.

Lucia chuckled.

"An angel? Really?"

"An Angel of Death, actually," I added.

"*Oh*," she continued, with her eyes lit and her teeth showing. "*Our Angela* is an Angel of Death? *Our Angela*, who chickened out when we ordered her to shoot who she thought was a traitor? Why should we believe she, of all people, was hand-picked to take lives?"

82

There were a few uncomfortable laughs around the room.

"Who knows?" I asked. I guess it didn't make much sense to me either. "You're right. It doesn't make any sense now that I've found *this* out. Maybe it's because *God* wants her to do it this time around instead of just some gang members."

This didn't sit well with Lucia.

"Well, think about it," I continued. "She literally found out that He wants her to do this. *Him*, the man upstairs. First of all, it's not like she can even say 'no' to Him. If He wants you to do something, I'm pretty sure you're doing it. I doubt there are any ifs, ands, or buts about it. Secondly, she's not exactly doing anything wrong if He's the one having her do it, right?"

Lucia didn't nod, but a few of the other girls did.

"Do you want to know how I personally know this is the truth?" I asked.

"Don't tell them, Shawn," Angela pleaded. "We know at least one of them is a Satan recruit whether she knows it or not. And, if she knows you'll be…"

I motioned for her to relax.

"How?" Lucia asked, glancing over to where Angela was standing. I definitely had her on the ropes now.

"Because I literally witnessed her walk into my grandfather's room and take his life with a simple kiss." Lucia's eyebrows arched; it was time for the kicker. "And this was after I watched her absolutely beat the snot out of two hulking dudes in front of three or so bystanders who didn't notice a thing. They didn't just ignore the commotion, mind you. They flat out didn't see it. And, just so you know, those two hulking dudes were Angels of Death as well, but they were working for Satan. So, Angela is the real deal. Trust me."

"Just don't tell them about the one outside," she pleaded, again.

"I won't," I mistakenly blurted out.

"You won't what?" Lucia asked, with definite fear in her eyes. Perhaps it was my mention of Satan that put it there, or she thought I was even crazier than before.

"I won't… I mean, *we* won't give up on you," I said. "I know this is a lot to have to take in all at once. There has to be a reason He chose Angela for this, though, and we think it's you girls."

"Well, how come *you* need to do all of the talking for her?" she asked. "Why can't *we* hear her? Or see her?"

She re-directed her attention to where Angela was standing. Man, how was I supposed to explain this without giving myself away?

"Look, I know this is all so mind-blowing," I said, hoping this would suffice. "It's probably even more so for all of you, considering she was your friend. But…"

"Right," agreed Lucia. "So, again, why is it she'll talk to *you*, but not us?"

I looked to Angela for any sort of help here, but alas, only the truth would do. Remember, she couldn't lie, nor could she suggest lying, I imagine. Asking me to lie on her behalf might have been worse than committing the sin herself.

"Because I'm dying," I finally admitted. I still hadn't gotten used to saying this yet; understandable, I think. "I know this sounds weird, but you should be happy you can't see her or speak with her."

It was dead silent in there for a couple of minutes. Lucia, who had daggers in her eyes for me earlier, now looked like she felt sorry for me; her eyes were an easy read. She was an emotional young woman. She'd seen a lot for a kid her age; I could tell.

"She told you this?" she asked, just to make sure. "Or did you just come up with it on your own?"

"*She* told me," I answered.

"Did she say when?" was her follow-up question.

I shook my head. "And, before you ask, she doesn't know where or how either."

84

"Are you scared?" a tiny voice asked. I couldn't tell where it came from initially. Then, one of the girls stepped forward and maneuvered her way around Kiki. There was definite concern in her eyes, only it wasn't there for me.

"At first I was," I began. "But once I came to grips with the fact that there was nothing I could do about it, I... well, I wouldn't say I've *embraced* it by any stretch, but I have accepted it. It's definitely a scary thing, without a doubt. I'd be lying if I said otherwise."

She nodded solemnly.

"Okay!" Lucia broke in, flustered. Things were clearly getting away from her. "Well, um, I really don't know what to do with all of this right now. Obviously, there's some craziness going on here, and I don't really know how to handle it, so I guess I should focus on what I do know how to handle: gettin' some revenge."

"*Revenge?*" Angela asked.

"Revenge for what?" I added.

Suddenly, it dawned upon me. "For Angela."

"Yeah," Lucia answered. "Of course. What do you think?"

I quickly looked to Angela, who was shaking her head frantically. We should have seen this coming, but I guess we were too caught up in everything else to consider it. This was what happened when major things moved rapidly.

"She doesn't want that!" I exclaimed. "She's shaking her head."

"Yeah, well, I'm sorry, girl, but this is how we do things," Lucia explained, glancing around the room and even up at the ceiling corners for some reason. Then she looked to me. "She knows this."

The girl who asked me whether or not I was scared looked mighty frightened herself now. She had the hopeless eyes going, wide and worried, when suddenly she pointed to the front doorway in a panic.

"*There she is!*" she screamed. "*Ay Dios mio!* Look at her! She's beautiful; she looks like a real angel."

We all quickly shifted our gaze to the doorway, even Angela herself, who we were supposedly looking at. What the hell was going on here?

"Am I the only one who can…" the girl continued.

We all interrupted her, nodding. Luckily for her, nobody noticed I had joined in. This was nothing more than a ruse.

"No!" she cried, but it didn't sound all the way genuine. "Then, this means…"

Lucia approached her and pulled her in for the kind of hug only a protective, older sister can typically deliver, if television is any indication. I could tell just by looking at her expression that the girl felt a little guilty now, wrapped in Lucia's embrace. She didn't speak up, though, so she mustn't have been *that* beat up over it; I guess I couldn't blame her.

"It's okay, Lil' Marie," Lucia said. "You can hang back. We're not going to let anyone take you away from us tonight, okay?"

Marie nodded. She forced the issue a little with a shiver. Talk about thinking on your feet, though. I mean, at times, I can be as cowardly as the next guy, and I doubt I would have thought of this.

"I think you should all hang back tonight," I blurted out.

Lucia wasn't pleased. I could tell she'd had enough of me, even if I was there on behalf of a higher power.

"Look, white boy," she began, pointing her finger in my face. She was just about touching my nose with her fingertip, but at least it wasn't the barrel of her gun this time around. "I get why you're here and I feel for ya, but we gotta go do us, aight? If we don't, this'll get out and people will think we're soft. I ain't for that. Now, you can hang here with Lil' Marie if you want, but the rest of us are out."

"Listen, who cares what anyone else thinks?" I naively asked. "This is bigger than all of that."

"That's easy for you to say," Lucia joked. "*This* is all we have. Society wants it this way. We're used to it. They don't expect us to do anything worthwhile for the world. They probably think the only positive thing *we* can do for it is put more kids like us in the ground."

"They've got Satan talking to them," Angela mentioned.

"Really?" I responded, shifting my focus to her.

"Yup," she said, matter-of-factly. Nothing involving Satan had ever come across as a matter of fact to me before; it was pretty unsettling, really. "Whenever you start telling yourself you're no good for whatever reason, it's *his* voice you're hearing. You should use this, Shawn. It's good stuff."

"What is she saying *now*?" Lucia asked, clearly a little miffed.

I didn't call her on this, though. I'm not sure "miffed" was the best word to describe her with if I liked my face intact. Just because she hadn't made an example of me yet didn't mean she wouldn't.

I myself was beginning to grow a bit miffed, or rather frustrated, with Lucia. She was a real pain in the neck. If what Angela said was true, which I'm sure it was, then she was putting a lot of stock in what Satan had to say, and in turn, the rest of the Destinas were most likely doing the same with what she had to say.

This, of course, begged the question: was the angel we encountered out in the front yard there for Lucia?

"Um, she's saying Satan's been talking to you."

"Really?" Lucia asked. "And, how exactly has he been doing that? This oughta be good."

She looked to the others to see if they were just as amused by this latest revelation. They weren't. At least, they weren't as bold about it as she was.

"*Oh, come on,*" she continued. "You're not really buying all this bull, are ya? You really think Satan's been hitting us up?"

"Not directly," I interrupted. "At least, this is my take on it: whenever *any* person – whether he be me, you, or whoever – starts getting down on himself, that's Satan talking to him. Understand? He wants you to

87

feel worthless or bad or whatever. I fall for it all of the time, too. It isn't as uncommon as we probably think.

"And that's not all. I'll bet he's also talking to every person out there who has written you girls off already. He's scared them away from seeing whatever good you can do. And if you keep on doing the kind of thing you probably have planned for tonight, then they're never gonna see your potential. They're always gonna be afraid of you. You'll be nothing but a dangerous group of gangsta girls to them. This is how he wins.

"Now, what I'm about to say might get me beaten to a bloody pulp, but I'm gonna say it anyways. I can personally admit I've never given the gangstas of the world much of a chance, and I've never placed the blame on Satan. This was a mistake on my part. I listened to him when I shouldn't have."

"What should we do then?" she asked. "Turn our back on the game and start doing *nice* things like fundraisers or whatever?"

"You joke, but why not?" I replied. "I'm telling you, you definitely have it in you. You can be good."

She started huffing and puffing. I stood my ground, though, when I normally would have backed down a little. I was notorious for planting seeds and just leaving them there under the dirt, unattended.

"Yeah, well, if He cares so much about us, then why have we been dealt such a lousy hand?" she asked. "I mean, look around. Where are Kiki's folks? Sorry, Kiki. I didn't mean to blow up your spot. It's just that this *gringo* here..."

I slowly began shaking my head, feeling very uncomfortable, and even a little spoiled, to tell the truth. "I don't…"

"*Neither does she,*" she interrupted me. "We know her old man's behind bars, but we don't know where those bars are. It ain't like it matters, though, because we know where he *ain't*; he ain't here. And then there's her mother. Where the hell is she? We haven't heard from her in days. *Days.* If this is Satan's doing, then I'll tell you what, that G is good at what he does. Just look at poor Kiki; she's tougher than she should have to be."

I had no choice but to steal a glimpse at Kiki. She looked strong enough to me, but I'm willing to bet at least some of that strength was little more than a façade put there because it needed to be there in her type of environment.

"I'm sorry, Kiki," I apologized. "It isn't fair, nor is it easy, but sometimes life is neither of those things. At least, this is how I…"

"Her family life is chips," Lucia interrupted. "What would *you* know about any of that? Where are *your* parents? At home, eating a lobster dinner or whatever white folks eat for dinner?"

I tried to remain calm. After all, she had no clue as to what I'd been through. All she knew was I was dying, and to her credit, she'd definitely been sympathetic regarding this matter, but she had no idea my parents were already there, waiting for me.

"Actually, they're dead," I said. "Both of them. Car accident."

I could tell she suddenly felt like a female dog. She shouldn't have, though. Barring my unfortunate circumstance, she probably would have been right on the money with her assumption. Mom and Dad did like their lobster, that was for sure. They used to check the supermarket flyers every Sunday for any upcoming deals.

"And now, you're dying," she reminded me, with sympathetic eyes.

"They're in a better place," I finally admitted out loud. I thought it would take me much longer to utter those words.

"Sometimes, I wish mine were, too," Kiki said.

She spoke slowly. Her immediate reaction told me she wasn't all the way sure she wanted to say what she said. It must have been a difficult thing to say, especially if she meant it wholeheartedly.

Poor kid.

I could say that and not feel guilty because I was probably one of the few people out there who had it far worse than her. I'd been putting up with the short end of the stick for so long that I no longer pitied myself. I was on to other people now.

Nobody called her out on wishing her parents dead. This unfortunately spoke volumes for them. Angela didn't even bat an eyelash.

"Tell them you'll take Lil' Marie's place in the whip," Angela said.

I looked at her incredulously. *"They're still going?"*

She nodded.

"Yeah," Lucia confirmed. "We're dippin', now."

"I… um... I'm coming," I said. "Angela wants me to take Lil' Marie's place in the car, I guess."

"Hey, it's on you," Lucia responded, shrugging her shoulders. "I'm good with it."

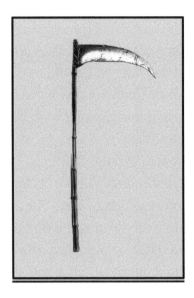

<u>Chapter 7</u>
Angela

I was a little surprised Lucia let Shawn tag along.

It wasn't like her, but, then again, I guess it made sense for her to be somewhat off-kilter after all that had gone on. Anybody would have been.

It had to have been like one of those moments when everyone realizes a divine intervention just took place; it takes a while to get back to being you.

Once we reached Rivers Street, I grew nervous – for all of us.

I figured I'd be put to the test once I set eyes on the girls who had probably gunned me down. I knew I wasn't expected to hold any sort of a grudge against them and I had already preached to Shawn that I wasn't angry with them, but this was before I really had the opportunity to see them in person.

Until then, they were nothing more than an SUV slowing down with a few guns firing out the side, so I could easily pin it on Satan; there wasn't anything human about them yet. I was far more concerned with this than I was with another possible encounter with one of his angels. So far, I had done pretty well against them.

When it came to Shawn and the Destinas, I'd say I was more confused than concerned. I still didn't know under what circumstances he'd be dying, nor did I know which of them the angel from Kiki's front yard was there for; nothing really ever came of that – not one clue.

When Lucia neared the Rivers Street Girlz's joint, the girls pulled their bandanas out and tied them around the bottom half of their faces, then they readied their nines. Shawn was as nervous as I'd ever seen him, and I thought nothing would have topped his reaction to hearing Satan was amongst us instead of below us.

"Why do you girls want to do this?" he asked. "Angela has already forgiven them. She seriously has."

In the rearview mirror, I could see Lucia rolling her eyes. They really stood out above the bandana; her make-up helped. She must have regretted allowing him to ride with them.

"We don't *want* to do this," she explained. "We *have* to do it. Now, I've already told you why, so don't bring it up again or else I'll personally be able to tell you when, where, why, and especially *how* you'll die. Feel me?"

Upon saying this, she placed her nine atop the dashboard. This was just for show, though. I knew this because she quickly grabbed it again and stuffed it down beside her somewhere.

"Okay," he said. "There's nothing more *I* can do, I guess."

He looked to me, the sly little punk.

"Not tonight, at least," Lucia added.

Well, I suppose it was somewhat reassuring to hear Lucia might need him going forward. I'll be honest with you; this was more than I was expecting.

"*Not tonight*?" he asked, again looking to me. This time, he offered me a pleasantly surprised expression. "Does this mean I have some sort of a future with the Destinas?"

Lucia didn't respond. A couple of the girls shifted their focus to him, but remained silent as well.

She quickly killed the lights, placed her free hand behind the passenger seat and gave us – well, them – a once over.

"Okay, girls, this is it," she said so calmly it sort of frightened me. "Don't wait for my word. When you see your shot, take it. You, stay down no matter what."

Shawn was way ahead of her; he'd already begun sliding down in his seat. Well, he slid as far as he could. They were pretty packed in back there.

The closer we got to the crib, the further down the windows slid into the passenger side doors. It was so quiet in there you could hear the glass sliding against the hard rubber as it disappeared. I never figured I'd consider this sound so ominous.

We slow rolled to a stop, during which time the girls drew their nines and readied them – barrels aimed out the car windows in the direction of the house. I'm still not sure which Destina fired first, but it didn't matter because they all began firing before long. Even Lucia snuck a few shots off before chirping them. As we pulled away, I could hear a flurry of curse words ringing throughout the house. It was something else, and not in a good way.

"Well, we definitely aired it out," Lucia began. "So, we had to have at least clipped one of them."

"We'll find out soon enough, I bet," Kiki said.

Every *chica* in the backseat placed her nine at her feet, which was probably for the best considering they still looked to be running on adrenaline. I know my hands always used to get jittery whenever I was that worked-up; in fact, I used to get the snaps – that is to say I snapped a lot when it happened.

You can't get like that with a nine in your hand.

"Did they fire back at all?" asked Rosa, the girl whose new Timbs nearly did irreparable damage to my face during the first stage of my initiation. I hadn't forgotten.

"No, they didn't," Shawn answered, still slumped down.

"What do you know?" Lucia barked. "You were practically lying down back there."

"*You* told me to stay down," he responded, huffing and puffing. "Remember?"

She rolled her eyes as she shook her head, and then checked her hair in the rearview. I guess I'd have been annoyed with him, too, if I had been her.

"Yeah, well, it doesn't matter whether or not they fired back *tonight*," she continued. "They're the ones who struck first. *Remember?*"

We weren't at Kiki's ten minutes before they came barreling onto her front lawn – *they* being the Rivers Street Girlz. Almost instantly, there were weapons drawn all over that yard.

"Yo! We know it was you!" shouted Ponnleu from the driver's seat. She was their leader.

"Of course it was us," Lucia responded, aiming her nine directly at her. "And we know it was you who tried to air this place out the other night."

"You clipped one of my girls tonight," Ponnleu said. "Did we clip any of yours?"

"*Pretty much!*" Lucia shouted, with her voice nearly cracking. "You clipped an innocent. She was a real good friend of ours."

"*Damn*," Ponnleu groaned. "Sorry, girl, for real. There's no way we could've known your friend was here."

"I know," Lucia said. "You still could've clipped one of us, though. I mean, that's why you were here."

"We needed to do it," she said. "You know that."

"*Si*," continued Lucia, morosely.

"So, what happens now?" Ponnleu asked.

"Well, for starters, I say we leave the hammers out of this one," Lucia suggested. Hammer, by the way, was what *she* called a gun. I hardly ever heard her use "nine" anymore.

The driver's side door opened slowly so as not to startle any trigger-happy Destinas, and Ponnleu finally slid out from behind the wheel. Clearly, she was still a little suspicious of Lucia's intentions, but she did at least have her nine pointed at the lawn.

"You go first, girl," she said.

Lucia appeased her, placing her gun down on the front steps, pointed away from the car. She motioned for the others to do the same, and they did. Some of them moved at a snail's pace, while still keeping an eye on the Rivers Street Girlz.

"So, no bloodshed tonight, then?" Ponnleu added, a little apprehensive herself.

"I didn't say all that," Lucia answered.

She took a few steps toward the car, with the remaining Destinas falling in behind her; it sort of took on a whole leading-the-sheep-to-the-slaughter feel. I grew a little nervous. It seemed like things were about to get real. Lil' Marie emerged from the crib to join them; I'd forgotten all about her.

Suddenly, the remaining three doors of the car swung open (a little too abruptly for my nerves) and the rest of the Rivers Street Girlz stepped out, thankfully empty-handed.

Lucia made her way out to the middle of the front lawn, eyeing Ponnleu the entire way.

"So, I guess you and *I* are gonna get things poppin'?" Ponnleu asked.

Lucia simply shook her head, as if to say, "I'm ready for whoever." She didn't care who she fought. She just didn't like waiting too long for her – or him in some instances. I'd seen her wipe a few dudes at school.

A lot of kids witnessed this; maybe this was why nobody was quick to meet her out there.

Finally, foolishly, Ponnleu sprinted over to Lucia. I figured Lucia would mop her right away, or at the very least, be the one to take the fight to the ground. Surprisingly, though, I was wrong.

She threw two quick slaps at Lucia's head. Neither one of them did any real damage, but the second one bought her enough time to grab hold of Lucia's hair and rip her down to the ground.

She followed with a kick to Lucia's left-lower back. Lucia grunted. At least she didn't scream. For some reason, *that* would have been disastrous.

Ponnleu tried to follow it with a punch to Lucia's side, which struck me as odd since I think I would have gone for her head. Luckily, it looked like she only connected with her tee.

Lucia took advantage of her mistake, grabbing hold of her wrist and wrenching her to the ground. I think she might have dislocated her shoulder. Unlike Lucia, though, Ponnleu couldn't suppress her scream.

She was clearly favoring her left arm, clutching the wrist with her other hand. Big mistake – even if it was hurting something fierce. Lucia punched her in her injured shoulder, probably as hard as I'd ever seen her punch anyone – including the boys I mentioned earlier.

Ponnleu was still in the fetal position on the lawn when Lucia got to her feet. She didn't take a breather at all, not even for a second. She started kicking Ponnleu all over – even trying for her face a few times, but fortunately failing to connect.

I tensed up each time I thought she was going to get her. I wasn't rooting for Ponnleu or anything; I just didn't want to see anyone kicked in the face. It's a pretty violent image – about as violent as it gets without using any weapons, I think.

Before I knew what happened, just about everyone was fighting. Shawn, and I think Lil' Marie, were the only ones who weren't. She was in the mix, but she didn't seem to be punching anyone or taking any punches. She was sort of just there.

It didn't take too long for everyone to gravitate to the middle of the lawn. They kept backing up toward and eventually brushing up against one another, which was sort of weird – only because I wouldn't have wanted to get too close to anyone else if I was in one of the fights.

It would have been enough for me just to worry about the fists *I* was up against.

As it turned out, the one I'd be up against showed up a short time later. He was smaller than all of the other angels I'd faced. This didn't mean much, though. I mean, look at me. I'm petite, but I had definitely held my own so far.

He was an angry little guy, not cocky like the others. I believe they call it Napoleon Complex or something along those lines. He marched right over to me, with his fists clenched. The only other image that would have fit right into the equation would have been him rolling his sleeves up.

I wish this hadn't popped into my head because I smirked, which probably only angered him further.

Just when I thought he was going to call me on it, he punched me in the face. I think the main reason I was ill-prepared for this was because I neglected to make the distinction between male angels and their human counterparts. Most men wouldn't strike a woman – or at least not with such force and disregard for how it made them look to others.

He floored me, figuratively *and* literally. Then, he mounted me and went right for my throat, squeezing like he knew for sure he'd lose if I'd gotten free.

I couldn't breathe, which I figured was something I didn't need to worry about anymore, but I was weakening. Surprisingly, the thing that snapped me out of it was the look on Lucia's face. She saw us – both of us.

"*Angela*?" she asked. "He was right?"

97

I nodded as best I could. Seeing how I struggled, she redirected her attention to him.

"*Get off of her*!" she shouted, then started toward us.

He grinned as he waited. She was his, I realized. I was confused. I mean, what was I supposed to do at that moment? Was this pre-determined, out of my control? The look in his eyes pissed me off enough to throw caution to the wind and step in.

"*Not gonna happen*!" I shouted, before throwing a punch where his heart should have been. Nothing.

"*Ahh*!" A shout came from my left, startling me. It was Lucia. I just knew it.

She was on her knees, with a knife somewhere in her back. She was whimpering, trying desperately to reach for it. When she came up short, she kept looking to all of the other Destinas for help. They were too busy to notice. I looked everywhere for Lil' Marie, but she was nowhere to be found.

Where was she? Lucia needed her.

The angel climbed off of me once it looked like Lucia was fading. He hurried over to where she knelt. All she could do was look up at him with fear in her eyes. Luckily, he was conceited enough to stare at her for a moment; clearly this was the type of moment this little man had been waiting a while for.

Well, he'd need to wait longer because I was now able to take advantage of the cockiness he hadn't shown me before. I threw him up against the Rivers Street Girlz's ride, knocking him unconscious for the time being.

I knelt down before Lucia, so we were at eye level. Hers were filled with tears; she couldn't believe what she was seeing. Blood began to trickle from her mouth. I didn't have time to go back and forth on this.

"I'm sorry, girl," I apologized.

Her eyes widened; she was, naturally, confused. I gently took her head in my hands and kissed her on the cheek, like she had done for me so

98

many times before. She fell forward into my arms, and I guided her to the ground.

I didn't worry about the commotion still raging around us. She was safe now.

The fighting died down once everyone noticed Lucia lying motionless on the ground with the knife still in her back. Lil' Marie, much to everyone's surprise, hurried right over to her.

"No, Marie!" Kiki blurted out. "Your prints."

Lil' Marie only scowled at her.

"I don't give a damn about my prints!" she shouted. "*It's Lucia!*"

She desperately tried to pull the knife out a couple of times, but was met with too much resistance. Rigor mortis must have set in; this seemed way too early for that, though. By the looks of things, everybody else must have felt the same.

Lil' Marie's brave face suddenly gave way to that of a frightened little girl. Her fingerprints were now all over the handle. She'd incriminated herself, big time.

The angel I thought I'd defeated rose to his feet.

Meanwhile, Marie was back at it, trying to move the knife around, no doubt hoping to jar it loose.

"Don't worry," he suggested, striding toward her. She didn't notice. She just kept wiping. Poor Marie.

My focus continuously jumped between them until it was broken by Shawn, whom I'd honestly forgotten all about.

"*Stop him, Angela!*" he shouted. "What are you doing?"

I snapped out of it and quickly speared him back into the hood of the car; I was using their car a lot that night. This was apparently the last I'd need of it, though, for he fell limp when a part of it – possibly the hood ornament – lodged in his back.

I spun around to find Lil' Marie staring directly into my eyes. She couldn't get over it; I could tell.

"*Angela*?" she asked, as wide-eyed as could be. You never saw someone so surprised in your life. I probably saw way more of her eyes than anyone ever had. "It's really you."

Once everyone realized something strange was happening – they still didn't know for sure what it was – the fighting ceased. As far as I know, Shawn and now Lil' Marie were the only ones who could see me. I glanced back at the car, and the angel was no longer there. I panicked, scanning the yard for him, but coming up empty.

Where is he? I thought. *I mean, where exactly do they go after I finish them off?*

Lil' Marie touched me, which completely caught me off guard to the point that I instinctively grabbed hold of her wrist and gave it a quick, inward twist. I thought it might have been him, coming back for more.

I quickly released her. I guess she was just having a moment; understandable.

"Wait! She can see you, too?" Shawn asked, concerned.

I nodded, without saying a word just yet.

"Then, how come she couldn't see you before?" he continued. "This doesn't make any sense."

"I don't know," I said, eyeing her confusedly – not quite suspiciously. "I'm guessing her threat level might've gone up since all of this has happened. Maybe the Rivers Street Girlz aren't finished with them yet? I don't know. I'm not sure how this all works yet."

He nodded, some of the concern disappearing from his face.

I took a moment to check on the Rivers Street Girlz to gauge what kind of threat they posed. They no longer seemed too aggressive to me; far from it, in fact. I think they were too blindsided by everything that had gone on.

On a night when they'd agreed to leave their nines out of it, I'm sure any one of them losing her life – least of all a leader – came as a complete shock. I know *I* didn't see it coming.

I just figured they'd be bangin' out and that'd be it. Live to fight another day, you know? Now, I wasn't stupid enough to think they'd be squashing it, but Lucia being killed? *That* surprised the heck out of me.

I guess I shouldn't have been all that surprised he was here for her, though, considering some of the stuff she'd been involved in. Still, she was my girl and I *had* seen a lot of good in her over the years.

We figured one of Kiki's neighbors must have called the boys because we heard sirens approaching. They were probably a few streets over when I first thought I heard them. In our neighborhood, they could have been going just about anywhere – not necessarily coming to break up whatever we had going on – but neither crew took any chances.

"This isn't over, you know!" Ponnleu shouted, as she filed into the car with the others.

"Not even close!" Kiki shouted back.

As the Rivers Street Girlz backed off of her lawn and sped away, Kiki and most of the surviving Destinas started for the safety of her house. The first one in killed all of the lights.

Meanwhile, Lil' Marie hung back, trying desperately to use the lower half of Lucia's tee to wipe her prints from the knife handle.

Shawn and I could only look on, a little worried for her. She wasn't able to do too thorough a job because she was interrupted when Kiki poked her head out.

"Lil' Marie!" she shouted, though it was kind of like one of those whisper shouts, if that makes any sense. "Get in here! They're coming!"

Lil' Marie shot her a frustrated glare.

"I can't!" she shouted back. "My prints are still on the handle."

"Forget about that," Kiki said. "They can't find any of us here. So, get inside!"

Kiki pointed behind her, with the intensity you'd think she'd been saving for her own misbehaving kids someday. Lil' Marie followed orders, and we followed her inside. Judging by her reaction, Kiki had forgotten all about Shawn in the heat of the moment; he understood.

With the lights off, it wasn't too easy to see where we were headed, so Kiki ushered us down to the basement. Lil' Marie kept stealing glances back at me the whole time.

We braced ourselves for the impending knock at the door, even though none of the girls had any intention of answering it. After a little while, we couldn't hear the sirens at all; they mustn't have been for us.

This was obviously a relief. We quietly made our way back upstairs.

We all stood at Kiki's picture window for what seemed like forever. Time had stopped for us in there. We were staring out at my departed friend and their fallen leader. There were tears – plenty of them. Lucia would have disapproved, but she wasn't around to do anything about it.

"Well, I guess we're all yours now, girl," Rosa said, placing her arm around Kiki's waist. "Treat us right; follow her lead."

I could tell Kiki didn't want this; not yet at least.

"Well, the first thing we need to do is get Lil' Marie somewhere where she can lay low for a while," she announced.

She then turned to Lil' Marie with sympathetic eyes. "Sorry, girl, but it's for the best."

Lil' Marie nodded. What else could she honestly do at that point?

Kiki continued. "Once we know for sure we're good, we'll try to get out there and wipe down that handle. But we still shouldn't take any chances. I mean, the boys might have some crazy CSI type stuff they can use on it."

"Well, yeah, but when are they even gonna see it?" Lil' Marie asked.

"After we figure out what to do with you, we're gonna call the boys ourselves."

They all looked at Kiki like she had two heads.

"Are you *loco*?" Rosa quickly asked, sounding concerned that she may have spoken too soon before.

"Well, I mean, it's not like any of us killed her," Kiki continued.

"*I know, but…*" Rosa pressed.

"What *should* we do then? Bury her somewhere like she wasn't our girl?"

I could tell nobody wanted to answer this; they all sort of looked down at the floor. Kiki was clearly the right choice for successor.

She checked things out the best she could one more time from the window. She mustn't have seen anyone out there, so she waved everyone toward the door. This was all so surreal to me, which, of course, was kind of a funny thought considering all *I* had been through.

"I think we're good," she said as we scurried by.

It was pretty eerie stepping out onto that lawn with Lucia's body still lying there right out in the open. For them, the night was probably still one big blur, but I oddly enough felt like it had been a while since I gave her that kiss.

I did a good job laying her down; I noticed that. She looked about as peaceful as a person probably could who had suffered a death so violent.

We all approached her body solemnly, as though it were her casket. I don't know how to explain it; this was honestly how it felt. The main difference between this and a typical wake – other than the obvious, I mean – was I had forgotten to shut her eyes. They looked just as they had when she found out for sure I was amongst them.

Kiki knelt before her fallen predecessor, pulled Lucia's bandana from her back pocket and proceeded to wipe the handle with it. I think she did a pretty thorough job. Lil' Marie was relieved, though she didn't show it.

"I'm sorry, girl," Kiki uttered. "This isn't how I…"

She broke down, unable to finish. I wanted to give her some moral support, but ultimately fought off the urge to place my hand upon her shoulder for fear that it might have triggered something.

I still wasn't altogether sure of what I could and couldn't do. Fortunately, Rosa stepped in to do what I couldn't risk.

Kiki gripped her hand without looking up at her; all she did was feel her hand sort of like *mi abuela* used to whenever I'd sit with her. The Destinas definitely loved one another. This exchange was all the evidence you'd need.

"Okay," Kiki finally said, following a deep breath. Back to business. "What are we going to do with you, Lil' Marie?"

She wiped her eyes as close to dry as she could and stood up.

"She can come back to Shawn's," I suggested.

Both Shawn and Lil' Marie shot me a look.

"She can come back to *Shawn's*?" he asked, bug-eyed.

"Actually, that *is* probably a good place for her," Kiki agreed.

It was settled.

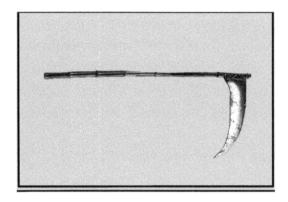

<u>**Chapter 8**</u>
Shawn

I guess this was like my take on the Bible in that if I was going to sign on for any of it, I'd sort of need to sign on for all of it, and that apparently meant letting a gangsta girl stay at my house while she was laying low on what could amount to a trumped-up murder charge.

This was how I'd be spending my remaining days? Harboring a soon to be fugitive? Seriously?

"Hey, it's not like she *is* a murderer, if that makes you feel any better," Angela said.

"*What*?" Lil' Marie blurted out.

"Oh, man, I forgot about that," I said.

I peered over at Lil' Marie. She was practically resting up against the passenger side door.

If she could have been outside of the car hanging on, then I think she would have been. She was positioned this way pretty much the entire drive to my house. It's funny; I would have figured a gang member – even a female one – would sit wherever the hell she wanted to in a dorky, white dude's car, but she looked more nervous than anything.

It probably had everything to do with the Angel of Death sitting in the backseat who she could now see and evidently hear and nothing to do with me.

"This *will* take some getting used to," I told Lil' Marie. "Everything, I mean."

She nodded.

"If you have any questions or anything, feel free, okay?" I added.

I figured this would help. I recalled how the news of my impending death first hit me. It was brutal.

"Hey, you have nothing to feel guilty about, Lil' Marie," Angela said. With my peripheral, I noticed her hand reach over and gently grip Lil' Marie's shoulder. Lil' Marie seemed startled to learn her thoughts were being heard.

Been there, felt that.

"Her death was imminent. There was nothing any of you could have done to prevent it, so please, stop shouldering the blame yourself. Okay, girl?"

Lil' Marie nodded, looking very nervous. Who could blame her?

"Nothing's gonna happen between us, you know," Lil' Marie was quick to point out to me. *This* was how she chose to change the subject.

Angela chuckled.

"Great," I grumbled. "I finally get to be with two women, but one can't and the other won't. He's killing me off and he can't even hook a brother up."

They both chuckled this time. I hoped my quip wasn't sacrilegious.

106

Not too far from home, I pulled into the first fast food joint we came to – it was one of the newer ones that laid claim to not only the freshest burgers but hand-cut fries as well.

I still didn't have anything worth eating at home. I could have just gone with a bowl of cereal, but I hate doing that. Besides, if my days were numbered, then I might as well eat like a king – or as close to royalty as I could get on my salary.

"So then, I guess this meal's on you, your highness?" Angela joked.

Lil' Marie was confused by our little *inside* joke.

I didn't want her to feel left out, so I engaged her. "Do you like their burgers?"

"*This place*?" she asked. "I've only been here like once or twice. They overcharge like crazy."

"Normally, I'd agree with you," I said. "But this is a special occasion."

"*Really*?" she asked. "What's the occasion?"

"We're dying," I said, probably a little too matter-of-factly for someone who had only just found this out about an hour or so earlier. To comfort her, I extended my fist for a pound. She left me hanging.

"Sorry," Angela apologized. "Don't worry. You'll get used to it."

"Get used to what?" Lil' Marie responded. "Death or his corny ass jokes?"

"Ah, back to the burgers," I suggested. "Since when do gang members concern themselves with something as miniscule as the price of a burger? Don't you people always have fresh *stacks* on you? Or… phat stacks or what have you?"

I tried to sound hip. Epic failure, apparently.

"We're not all trappers, you know," she fired back, clearly agitated.

"No. I know that," I said, trying to calm her down. "I didn't think you were *all* trappers, but… I mean…"

"So, what's a trapper, Shawn?" Angela asked. I found her smirking in the rearview. Man, if she wasn't an angel, then I might have flipped her off for blowing up my spot.

While I ordered the food, Lil' Marie kept checking on Angela, no doubt wondering what was taking her so long to decide what she wanted.

Once I'd completed the order and she still hadn't spoken up, Lil' Marie started probing.

"You're not hungry?" she asked, turning to face her.

"Not since that night," Angela responded.

"*Damn*!" was all Marie could say; it was actually kind of comical. "Is that what I have to look forward to? That sucks."

"Maybe," Angela answered. "I don't know."

Maybe? What about me? Was I going to be chosen to not be hungry?

"I… do… not… know," she repeated. I couldn't really tell whether or not she was just repeating what she'd told Lil' Marie – because people will sometimes do that to avoid an awkward silence – or if she was responding to my concern.

"So, I'm probably *not* going to be an angel?" Lil' Marie asked. I think she took offense to it. "Is that what you're saying?"

"No," Angela calmly replied. "I'm just saying I have no idea what His plan is. Nobody…"

"Wait!" she interrupted. "*Whose* plan? Who are you talking about?"

"God," Angela answered, incredulously. "This is all part of His plan."

"So, there really is a God?"

Well, this just blew my mind. I mean, how could a possible non-believer and I share the same status? Something didn't seem right here. I glanced into the rear view to find Angela offering me a reassuring look.

It's difficult to describe the look exactly, but it did the trick alright – it was very calming.

"How do you know?" Lil' Marie continued. "Have you seen Him with your own eyes?"

I thought his last question of hers came off as pretty condescending

"No," Angela said.

"See?" Lil' Marie responded, practically beaming.

"But, you see, I've never needed concrete evidence to believe in Him," Angela began. "And the way I see it, if my faith and belief aren't based upon this kind of evidence, there's no evidence you or anyone else will ever be able to produce that could cause me to question His existence. Ya feel me?"

Ooh! Marie got served. Still, she came back for some more.

"Well, what do you think His plan for you is?" she asked. "I mean, He made you an angel, so He must have something big planned for you, right?"

At first, I felt bad for Angela because I knew fully well she couldn't lie. In fact, I was going to interrupt them and get going on a new conversation to help her out of this, but it quickly dawned on me that this was something I kind of wanted to hear, too.

"I'll be helping in the next great battle for Heaven," she answered. "We'll be battling Satan's forces."

"*Satan's forces?*" Lil' Marie asked, struggling to withhold her laughter. "Wow! So, God wants *you* to fight against Satan and whoever's on his side? Stop selling 'em."

"This isn't a ticket," Angela began. "It's the truth."

Lil' Marie only shook her head, though; she was still fighting back that laughter.

"Well, then, you're *loco*," she added. "I mean, think about it. Why would He choose someone like you? What could *you* possibly do to Satan? This is stupid. It doesn't make any sense."

Angela didn't take this short; she was undaunted.

"I'm not who I used to be," she said. "Obviously." She tried to leave it at that – she really did.

"Okay, for argument's sake, let's say you *are* keeping it a hundred with me," Lil' Marie began. "You say this is the *next* great battle for Heaven?"

Angela nodded.

"Well, what happened the last time?" Lil' Marie added.

"Satan was cast out of Heaven."

"What started this *great* battle? Why was there drama between Satan and whoever?"

"Well, three things - the *whoever* was God. And Satan 'A' disagreed with the way He was running things, and 'B' thought too highly of himself," Angela said.

Angela was clearly agitated.

"So you can't have high self-esteem in Heaven?" Lil' Marie asked.

"Allow me to delve a little deeper into this for you," Angela began.

I could tell she was pissed that she needed to further explain this.

"In Satan's opinion, he was God's equal. In fact, he thought *he* should have been God."

"So, God decided Heaven wasn't big enough for both of them?"

"Well, yeah, but you're making it sound like God was being a tyrant or something."

"He wasn't?"

Angela shook her head in frustration. Who could blame her? Lil' Marie was being a real pain in the you know what. I personally didn't like where she was taking this conversation.

She kept right on pushing buttons with this nonsense even after we got home; she didn't give that mouth of hers a rest. I was getting ticked, but Angela was soon back to her typical, calm demeanor.

Seriously? Your girl here is taking it to the Lord, and you're fine with that?

"She isn't *taking* it to Him," Angela corrected. "She's just confused; that's all. She'll come around."

110

Lil' Marie shot me a look. Oddly enough, she didn't seem all that displeased with me for thinking behind her back.

"I forgive you, white boy," she joked. She hit me with a nod of acknowledgment. It was kind of weird receiving this from a girl.

I have to be honest, I was surprised at how quickly she made herself at home. I mean, not only was this going to be her new residence for God-knows-how-long, but she hadn't had that long to get even sort of used to all of this.

Things were no longer how they seemed in the direst of ways; depending upon your viewpoint, that is. I'm sure once you understand you're part of something divine, it's a lot easier to take in. Until then, it's a lot to have to cope with, and you aren't left with much time to do it.

She had very confident eyes now; I noticed that. I only say "now" because she didn't have them earlier. In fact, back when she was only pretending to see Angela, they were as nervous as any I'd seen. *What was it? What had changed?*

Maybe the difference between us was born of our environments; mine of the middle-class, typically safe for the most part, white suburbia, and hers of the always looking over your shoulder, poverty-stricken, even the cops are reluctant to drive through there unless they absolutely must, predominantly Hispanic ghetto.

"So, where am I staying?" she asked, following dinner. "Can you show me? I'm getting a little tired. Tonight's been a little… well, you know."

For some reason, I looked to Angela for her approval; why, I don't know. I was treating Lil' Marie like we had kidnapped her. Weird. Either that or maybe I was afraid she'd steal something if she was out of our sight, which, of course, was pretty foolish since she'd probably be living out the rest of her life there anyways.

"I still don't know why they chose Angela to be a freakin' Angel of Death," Lil' Marie blurted out on our way upstairs. I could tell it was festering. "She isn't for that life."

111

"Maybe she just wasn't 'for that life' down here," I said. I tried not to sound too smug about it. "Up there, it's probably a different story. She probably isn't taking lives so much as saving souls. So, yeah, she probably wasn't for that life, but God obviously thinks she's for that afterlife."

She rolled her eyes; I guess I should have expected that. Still, I couldn't tell if it was at the point I was trying to get across or the way I was trying to do it – with my unwarranted use of their vernacular. Even though we were close in age – I might have had her by a year or so – I felt like that father who tries to sound hip in front of his son's or daughter's friends. Ugh! I'd never felt so old in my life.

"Why are you still here?" she asked me.

"I live here," I answered matter-of-factly.

"Not for long."

She was right.

"Do you mean why hasn't she taken me yet?"

"No," she said. "I mean, why haven't you dipped? I'd have been outta here by now if I was you."

"Well, I could ask you the same question, couldn't I?"

"Not really." She arched her eyebrows, and took a step back, distancing herself from me. "I'm hiding from the boys. You're here by choice."

"Am I, though?" I asked. "I mean, if my impending death is part of God's plan, so much so that He introduced me to an Angel of Death ahead of time instead of just killing me off, then do you *really* think I have any choice in the matter?"

I could see her mulling it over.

"And, for the record," I continued. "I did try to ditch her, but it didn't pan out. I ended up talking myself right back into it, and it surprisingly didn't take me long at all to do it."

"Well, if you know you're gonna die soon and there's nothing you can do about it, then why don't you just hang it up and go out on your own accord?"

112

I couldn't believe she had suggested this. I wanted to give her an earful over it, but I couldn't really tell whether or not she was saying it just to be a you-know-what or if the poor thing really thought this was a good idea. *Was she herself suicidal?* Was this what she was telling me, in a roundabout way?

"Because I still have a reason to live," I finally said, hoping this would scare her away from this kind of thinking.

She only balked at this, though. "I don't get it."

"The way I see it, life is worth living if you have people you would die for," was how I explained it. I hoped this did the trick, because I didn't have much more to throw at her.

"Well, then, who are you dyin' for?" she pressed on.

"Everyone, I guess."

Now, I didn't know if this was true, but something or someone made me say it. I doubt I could have come up with it on my own. Then again, maybe Angela had rubbed off on me some.

"Ah, so you also think you're better than me," she said, not exactly hurt, though.

"No, I don't," I said. You see, unlike Angela, I still had a few lies left in me. "I just think our opinions differ big time on this."

"So, does this mean you're looking forward to death, on the off-chance that you too will be made an angel?" she asked.

I shook my head.

"I'm not looking forward to it," I answered. "But, at least, now I understand *why* it has to happen. Or at least I think I do. There's a certain amount of comfort in that. It softens the blow, if you know what I mean."

"If you say so," she added. She then rolled her eyes and shook her head.

While I showed her where everything was in the guest room- which was kind of pointless since we never really kept much of anything in there to begin with - she just sort of made herself comfortable on the bed. What I mean is she didn't just sit on the edge of the bed like I expected her to.

Instead, she scooted her way back so she was resting up against the headboard.

"Oh, okay," was all I really came up with for a response. It wasn't the best one, I'll admit that. "Yeah, just make yourself comf…"

"Thanks," she interrupted. "You know, you can chill for a while if you want. I was just messing with you in the car."

I needed to think for a minute. Oh yeah, she was talking about her no-funny-business prerequisite.

"Wait," I said. "So…"

She slid over a little to make room for me before I could finish my thought. She'd gone from wanting nothing to do with me to apparently wanting everything to do with me.

What was her game here? *Or was it even a game?* Perhaps it dawned on her that this might just be her last opportunity to have sex.

I'm not going to lie, I didn't rule it out, not completely anyways. After all, it was highly probable I'd never have this opportunity again either.

And, I mean, would it really have been out of wedlock if I wasn't even going to have the chance to get married? She had this devilish gleam in her eye as though she too had the ability to hear my thoughts.

I wasn't left teetering on the fence too long before the one I knew for sure could listen in on my thoughts made her presence known. Angela entered the room and immediately gave Lil' Marie a disapproving glance.

"What?" she asked, maneuvering over to the edge of the bed.

"Nothing," Angela sighed.

What else *could* she do? You couldn't really blame Lil' Marie for wanting to have sex before she died. I mean, even though it was doubtful, suppose she was still a virgin. My doubting this had zero to do with her environment. It had everything to do with the fact that I'd only had sex once up to that point.

It didn't take Angela too long to shift her focus to me; her demeanor didn't change any. I think she thought I was just as much to blame as Lil' Marie.

I widened my eyes, hoping this would quell those thoughts. It may have done just the opposite, though. I may have taken on that caught-red-handed look.

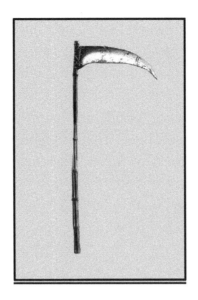

<u>Chapter 9</u>
Angela

I was relieved to discover this wasn't his doing. It was strange; he looked guilty and even felt guilty, but he wasn't guilty.

Marie quickly lost whatever respect she had for him; she thought he was whipped. I was surprised she didn't make that corny as hell whipping motion. Perhaps this was mostly a guy thing and not so much a girl thing.

Made sense, I guess.

There was an awkward silence, but it fortunately didn't last long. Lil' Marie's phone interrupted it; she had received a text.

"It's Kiki," she said, without looking up from the screen. "She wants the address."

Shawn hesitated. He wasn't too sure about this. One gangsta girl staying there seemed fair enough to him; now, he was worried his house was going to become the new Destina hang-out.

His grandfather would be rolling over in his grave. His thought, not mine.

"Don't worry, Shawn," I said, hoping this would comfort him enough. "Nothing's gonna happen. They like you, remember?"

"Twenty-seven Crenshaw Street," he reluctantly blurted out. She immediately typed it and sent it off.

I hated forcing him into this, but it'd be in our favor to have them here even if it was for just a little while. I mean, we honestly should have invited them sooner.

"They're on their way," Lil' Marie announced, shutting the phone off for the time being.

"*They are*?" he asked. "Already?"

She grinned, clearly enjoying his nervousness. He could wave bye-bye to his comfort zone. Wow! She thought this was great. I never realized she had such a mean streak to her; she never seemed it.

"Yup," she gladly responded.

"Why?" he continued.

"She didn't say, but it probably has something to do with either the Rivers Street Girlz or the boys."

"The cops?" he asked, too nervous to be impressed with himself.

"*Yeah*," she said. "The boys

He was definitely regretting his decision now. No good could come of either of these scenarios.

"Don't worry," I repeated, taking his hand in mine. I wasn't sure why I did this; it was something a girlfriend normally did. Lil' Marie noticed and then smirked, so I quickly let go of it, which probably didn't help my case any.

What was that all about? This was an earthly desire, wasn't it? I wasn't supposed to have those anymore; Michael said so. Or did he say I *shouldn't* have those anymore? I was definitely confused.

Come to think of it, though, I *was* a little jealous when I walked in on them. I didn't think anything of it at the time.

I had definitely surprised Shawn as well with this gesture. He quickly wrote it off, though, reminding himself I couldn't have been acting on an earthly desire because I didn't get those anymore. Phew! That was a close one. I thought I left myself wide open there, and he didn't capitalize.

I wish I could have said the same for her, but I found her eyeing me suspiciously as a result. She knew. He didn't notice her stare, I don't think. Unfortunately, his mind was back on my apparent PDA.

"Well, we should all head downstairs," I interrupted, before he had the chance to read too far into it. "It shouldn't take the girls too long to get here."

He sort of stumbled by me. He was nervous around me now; not a good sign.

We weren't downstairs long before the rest of the Destinas showed up. I wouldn't say they made themselves right at home, but they were a lot less nervous than they looked just before we split up.

"All this yours?" Kiki asked Shawn, point-blank.

"You tell me," he answered, not as punkish as I'm sure it sounds.

"Good answer," she said, and then pinched his cheek. He blushed a little, the pig. The funny thing, though, was for some reason I didn't mind when she did this. It wasn't like it was with Lil' Marie earlier. Kiki seemed safe.

We all filed into the living room. Kiki led the way even though it wasn't her house; I guess she banked on most living rooms pretty much being in the same spot. She had the right attitude, that was for sure.

She sat in the leather recliner I hadn't even sat in yet and I'd had a few days to do so. The rest of us just sat wherever. She wasn't as

119

intimidating as Lucia – not yet at least, but she seemed just as primed for the role as Lucia ever was.

Where Lucia seemed like the type to sit back and have everyone else figure things out for her, Kiki almost seemed like she didn't trust any of the others with her newfound responsibility. As bizarre as it sounds, she seemed like a little kid with a brand new, fragile toy.

"So, I'm thinking we need to come back hard after this," she said. "I mean, not to take anything away from the rest of us, but they did take out our leader. We can't take that short."

"But you killed one of them, didn't you?" Shawn asked.

He didn't get it.

Kiki looked pretty agitated with his interruption and even more so with his naivety.

"Yeah," she admitted. "But *that* was for Angela."

Both Shawn and Lil' Marie peered over at me. The others followed suit even though they couldn't have seen me.

"So, then, it just keeps on like this?" he asked, incredulously.

Kiki rolled her eyes, but nodded.

"Until what?" he continued. "Until none of you are left? Because look around. At this rate, it shouldn't take that long."

"Look!" she began. "If you're gonna be like this, then kick rocks. You shouldn't be here anyways. This is Destina business."

"*This is my house!*"

He stood up, then *they* stood up almost in unison, with Kiki leading the way. Rosa flashed her nine.

He took one look at it, then at them, and humbly sat back down. I felt bad for him, but he really should have known better.

It didn't take long for him to regret standing his ground and staying in the room. They got going on some pretty heavy stuff – revenge.

"The first thing we need to do obviously is figure out which one of them did it," Kiki began. "I didn't see *anything* unfortunately. And this isn't just what I'm gonna tell the boys. I mean, to keep it a hundred, I literally didn't see anything. One minute, she's wiping some chick, and the next thing *I* know, she's got a knife in her back."

She looked down at the floor. She did this a lot, I noticed, whenever her emotions were getting away from her.

"Did anybody see who shanked her?" she continued.

"Or even who they think did it? I mean, who knows? Maybe if we know for sure who we're after, they'll hand her over instead of having this go back and forth until we're all dead, like *he* said."

Shawn tried his best not to give her the *I told you so* look, but he failed miserably. In all fairness, though, she did catch him off-guard.

"Maybe we'll be good if we handle it like this," she continued. "So, anybody? Anything?"

They had nothing for her.

"What are you gonna do to her?" Lil' Marie asked. She was nervous; maybe she was in over her head.

"I don't know," Kiki answered. "But I have a few ideas. Dismemberment comes to mind."

What? Really? Yeah, I definitely wasn't cut out for this – pardon the pun.

"Dismemberment?" Lil' Marie asked. "What's *that*?"

None of the others seemed too eager to answer her.

"It's the reason I can't be in here anymore," Shawn spoke up.

"Congrats, Kiki. You got your wish. I don't know whether you're kidding or not, but I'm good either way. *Dismemberment? Seriously?*"

Shawn marched right out of the room en route to the kitchen. I joined him in there shortly thereafter. On my way out, I could hear Lil' Marie ask about dismemberment again.

"*Seriously*, what is it?"

"You really should be in there with them, Shawn," I suggested.

Before I could finish, he was already shaking his head.

"Look! I know I'd probably be dead before they locked me up for anything anyways," he began, "but I still don't want to be party to whatever she's planning."

I made the mistake of smirking. He was *so* worried about this that I couldn't help it.

"*Hey!* I'm serious!" he shouted, which in itself probably sounded pretty comical to everyone in the other room, aside from maybe Lil' Marie. Who knows, though? With this new mischievous side I never knew she had, she probably found it amusing, too, providing she wasn't still hung up on dismemberment.

"I know, and this is why now is the perfect time to get back in there and preach the Word to them," I explained.

"*Now?*" he asked, incredulously. "But… they're…"

"In desperate need of it," I interrupted.

He sighed.

"Maybe you're right," he finally admitted. "What should I…"

I produced his Bible from behind my back like it was some sort of a magic trick, and then handed it to him. I folded over a page I felt he should take a closer look at.

"I think John 5 will do for now," I suggested.

He opened to John 5 and got reading. He nodded once it hit him.

"Gotcha," he said, and then joined the girls.

I'll spare you the details of Kiki's plan for exacting revenge. Let's just say it involved kidnapping and the aforementioned dismemberment.

"Kidnapping, now?" Shawn asked. His voice had risen about two octaves.

Kiki, of course, rolled her eyes.

"Who let you back in?" she asked, clearly agitated.

Before he could respond, she spoke up again.

"Listen, Jiminy Cricket. We don't need you teaching us right from wrong. We don't. We know all this is wrong. We've *always* known it;

we're not stupid. But even though we've always known it, at the same time, it's all we know. Feel me?

"So, how you gonna expect us to just all of the sudden change it? Nah. We ain't about that. We can't be about that. It's too late; we need to do us."

"It isn't too late," Shawn came back with. "You girls are what? Eighteen, or somewhere around there?"

They nodded. Well, everyone except for Kiki and Lil' Marie.

"There once was a guy that had been sick for thirty-eight years," he continued. "He probably thought he'd never get better. Fair to say?"

Again, they nodded; still nothing from Kiki and Lil' Marie.

"Well, he was lying down next to this pool one day, and he couldn't get into it on his own on account of his illness. I'm not sure what it was. But he needed somebody to help him in, and nobody was around to hook a brotha up."

A few of the girls snickered. Something cool was happening, though. Somehow, aside from the two stubborn pains in the neck, they all started to look like little kids waiting to hear what happened next. They were definitely invested in the story.

"Anyways, *Jesus* himself sees him lying there and asks him if he wants to be healed. Naturally, the guy wants to be. I'm guessing the pool plays a big part in this; otherwise, why mention it, right?

"Anyways, the sick guy tells Jesus that he's got nobody to put him into the pool when the water is stirred up. Well, Jesus being Jesus looks at the guy and tells him to get up and walk."

Lil' Marie rolled her eyes, which pissed me off a little. She really needed to give it a rest.

"And, just like that," he said, snapping his fingers. "The dude gets up and walks. He's healed."

"What does this have to do with us?" Kiki asked, not really in a disrespectful way, though. Deep down, I think she wanted something to happen here.

"The guy probably thought he was stuck like this forever," Shawn guessed.

"I mean, why wouldn't he? It had been thirty-eight years since he first got sick. It probably got to the point where it was all *he* knew, and sadly, he probably accepted this fate. It all changed for him, though.

"It turned out the Lord hadn't forgotten about him. I guess He just hadn't gotten around to fixing him yet. And maybe He hasn't gotten around to fixing *your* situations yet."

They all grumbled for the most part.

"Until now, that is," he finally added.

"I'm guessing this is why He's sent Angela and me to help you. And, what I forgot to mention to you because I didn't want to lose you right away was that an angel descended from Heaven earlier on in the story to stir up the water in the pool. *An angel*! Think about it."

"That was a nice story," Kiki began. Just the way she said it I could tell she was about to take the momentum away from him. "But we're not really into the whole Jesus thing."

Thing? I was as perturbed as Shawn was confused.

"Wait," he began. "So, you're an atheist? Even after all..."

He motioned toward me, for in his mind I was all of the evidence any of them should have needed to know God existed.

"Now, I didn't say all that," Kiki pointed out, sort of defensively, if you ask me. "All I said was we're not into the whole *Jesus* thing."

He was still in disbelief, looking to me for some sort of help.

"Don't," a voice whispered in my ear; it was Michael's. I turned my head, but he was nowhere to be found. I definitely didn't imagine him, though, so I simply followed orders.

Shawn sighed when I had nothing for him.

"That's a shame," he said – to them, not me. "Because He was into the whole Destina thing. Actually, He was into the whole *humanity* thing – all of us."

"Yeah, so they say," Kiki fired back with. She wasn't letting up. I wanted to step in; I really did.

Shawn grinned, which was something I wasn't expecting at all. Perhaps it was the ridiculousness of the situation. He opened his mouth to counter what she'd said.

"Just because they say it," she continued, beating him to the punch. "That doesn't make it true. We don't know for sure He was the Son of God. At least, I don't."

He maintained his grin; I wasn't sure how. Apparently, he was beginning to appreciate the challenge.

"Well, then, for argument's sake, at the very least, there was a guy just over a couple thousand years ago who *thought* He was taking the mother of all beatings for you and He even made the ultimate sacrifice to keep you out of Hell.

"Shouldn't you at least do *your* best to stay out of there? I think that'd be a nice gesture."

Oh, I liked what I was hearing. Well played, Shawn, well played.

"We've all taken a beating for one another," Kiki explained. "So has Angela."

He glanced at me, somewhat confused.

"Oh, she didn't tell you about that?" she continued, practically grinning.

"Yeah, the first stage of her initiation was a beat down. We all wiped her. Being jumped in is a huge part of the Destina initiation. Hell, if Lucia hadn't stopped her in time, Rosa was gonna do some *serious* damage to Angela's face."

He looked to me again. I confirmed this with a nod.

Rosa looked over to where she figured I was; she was only off by a little bit. She was clearly nervous. She probably wasn't sure whether or not I was going to attempt to exact some revenge now that I'd been reminded of her role in all of this.

She had nothing to worry about. She was simply following orders we both knew she needed to follow.

"So, you all beat her up at the same time, or 'jumped her in,' or whatever you called it?" Shawn asked.

Kiki nodded.

"We jump in *and* we jump out," she added, sneering a little when she said it.

"Jump *out*?" he asked.

"Yeah," she answered, with obvious contempt.

"In other words, if anybody wants to willingly leave the Destinas, she needs to take another beating and you'd better believe it'll hurt a helluva lot more than the first beating."

He reluctantly nodded. He knew this latest bit of information could and probably *would* toss a huge monkey wrench into his plans for leading them each down a different path.

"Who was it?" asked Michelle, one of the typically less vocal Destinas.

"I'm sorry?" he replied.

"Who beat up Jesus?" she continued. I could tell she had a soft spot for Him.

"Oh, um, it was a few different people," he began. "First, it was His Jewish captors and a few Roman soldiers who went to the garden to find Him."

"*Jewish* captors?" she interrupted. "But I thought He was Jewish."

"He was," Shawn explained. "In fact, He was their king, chosen by God himself. I guess this wasn't a good enough endorsement for the high priests. They were pretty much the Jewish leaders. Other than Jesus, I mean. Actually, now that I think about it, it's no wonder they weren't too keen on the idea of Him being king."

"So, what happened after they got Him?" she asked.

"Well, His boy – maybe His right hand at the time – Simon Peter drew his sword and cut off one of His captors' ears. Jesus gave him a talking to for that, saying it was wrong and whatnot. Then, He healed the guy, which would have been enough for me not to bring Him in; I don't know about you. They *still* brought Him in, though, and He was totally fine with it."

"He was?" asked Rosa, now clearly intrigued. "*How? Why?*"

"Once again, He did it all for us," Shawn explained, practically beaming. He was starting to get excited, so much so that I was praying he wouldn't all of a sudden start tripping over his words. "Anyways, they brought Him before the high priests, roughing Him up a little along the way. Again, it was all good. He expected as much."

I loved the way he delivered the Word. He was very normal about it, very approachable, I guess. There was nothing condescending in what he said.

"What happened when He got to the high priests?" Rosa asked.

"Yeah?" Michelle added.

Shawn beamed; he knew he had them. He made sure not to grin or anything because something like that might have cost him his audience.

"Well, they asked Him a bunch of questions, trying to get Him to slip up so everyone would think He was full of it. He didn't, though, and this pissed them off even further.

"So, when that didn't work out so hot for them, they figured they'd bring Him to Pontius Pilate, the Roman prefect assigned to them. Basically, he was the guy in charge. He listened to what the high priests had to say and still didn't find all that much wrong with what Jesus was doing.

"He, at least, figured He didn't deserve to die over what they were saying about Him. In fact, Pilate was even going to let Him go. He said he'd either release Jesus or this horrible dude Barabbas, who I believe might have been what we'd consider a terrorist nowadays, and they chose to have Barabbas released.

"Can you believe that crap? *A terrorist*? Like the 9/11 guys."

127

The girls shook their heads, clearly disgusted. I reacted the same way the first time I heard it.

"I think even Pilate was dumbfounded," he continued.

"And Barabbas, too. That SOB probably thought he'd be crucified, which I believe *was* the plan. I'm pretty sure the only person who saw this coming was Jesus himself.

"I mean, it had to happen; it was God's plan and all."

"Was that when they hung Him on the cross?" Michelle asked, no doubt hoping the story was coming to an end.

Shawn shook his head for a few seconds before continuing.

"Not even close. You see, Pilate didn't want to kill Him, but he had to do something to appease the high priests, so he just had some of his men take Jesus outside in the public square – or whatever they called it – and do a number on Him. I guess his only order for them was 'Don't kill Him.' And they didn't, but, *man*, did they come close.

"They whipped Him until he bled. Then they caned the hell out of Him, and finally, they used this other kind of whip that had sharpened pieces of bone and iron woven into the straps. They literally tore the flesh from His body with this thing; they used it all over, even on His head.

"You would have thought they poured a bucket of crimson paint on the ground He bled so much. It was *bad*."

"*Stop*!" Michelle pleaded. She'd heard too much apparently. It looked like they all had, but only she spoke up.

"I'm sorry if I got a little too graphic there, girls," he apologized.

"I thought you could handle it, and I thought you should know exactly what He went through for you. Yeah, a lot of people know He died for our sins and was beaten like a dog up to that point and whatnot, but I doubt many of them know to what extent He was abused. With the exception of my grandfather and, of course, my parents, I doubt there's anybody I ever would have taken a beating like that for.

"I mean, even if you told me I was doing it to save the world, I still doubt I would've taken one for the team. It's just not who I am. I guess it's the biggest difference between Him and me.

"The good thing is I don't think God expects this of any of us. What He does expect, though – at least, I'm pretty sure of it – is that we honor His son's sacrifice by trying to live a sinless life. We all do things we know we shouldn't, but we figure it's all good because He did what He did for us. I know I do sometimes.

"And we can't really blame our environment or where we come from either. Because guess what? Nazareth was basically the hood. Nobody expected anything or anyone good to come from Nazareth, then, all of a sudden, Jesus *of Nazareth* shows up. Man, was that ever a jaw-dropper for people. Why couldn't you girls drop jaws, too?"

They all smirked when he said this.

"*Seriously*," he reiterated. "You could change *everybody's* perception of you if you really wanted to. The key component here, though, is *if* you wanted to. So, do you?"

Nobody answered him. A few of the girls actually looked like they were on the fence until they locked eyes with Kiki; they quickly dropped their look of uncertainty.

Kiki stood up.

"Lil' Marie, you need to stay here. The rest of you, let's dip."

"Well, that certainly could have gone better," Shawn said with a sigh.

He watched them through the window as they pulled away, bass pumping.

"You did fine," I said.

He rolled his eyes. He didn't agree with me.

"Um, why didn't you help me back there?" he asked me.

"Michael told me not to," I answered. "And he's kind of my boss, so I need to follow his rules."

"*Rules?*" he asked, incredulously. "I thought the only rules we needed to concern ourselves with anymore were like the Ten Commandments. I needed you back there; that wasn't cool, what you did."

"Did you really, though? I mean, didn't you see how captive your audience was? They were yours for the most part. I thought you did great, and Michael must have known you'd be great. Otherwise, I doubt he would have had me stay out of it. Think about it."

He did. Part of him was still a little heated at me, but the rest of him came around quicker than expected, so I knew it was just a matter of time.

"I think I'm going to head up to my room and get some reading done before I turn in," he announced.

"What are you reading?" I blurted out.

I wasn't sure why I asked. For starters, I obviously already knew. This was pathetic, but I think I only hit him with this question so he'd stay downstairs with us a little while longer.

"The *only* thing I read anymore," he replied.

The Bible.

"Yeah, I think it's time for us to have a little chat," Michael said. This time, I saw him. He was standing right next to me, watching Shawn drudgingly take the stairs.

Lil' Marie didn't even acknowledge Michael. Perfect. It'd be one less awkward moment for me. Sometimes, I was less than thrilled being a bridge.

"I'm going to turn in for the night, too," I said. She finally turned toward us – well, me.

"Alright, girl," was all she said.

"Need anything before I head up?" I asked.

She shook her head, and then plopped right down on the couch when we left, like she was beat.

Once in my bedroom, I turned and awaited Michael's word. Impressive. He didn't even look over at the bed. *There* was yet another difference between men and angels.

Not that I was a hottie by any stretch, but I'm willing to bet most men's eyes are immediately drawn to a woman's bed once they enter her room even if they have no intention of using it.

Apparently, this wasn't the case with angels.

"It definitely isn't," he quickly interjected. "Not with this angel, at least."

I blushed. With all of the thoughts I'd been reading lately, I'd forgotten just how vulnerable my own were.

"What's going on here, Angela?" he asked, clearly concerned. "You shouldn't be falling for him. We've gone over this."

"*I know*," I began, frustrated. "It's just that…"

"It can't happen," he interrupted.

"It can't because it will jeopardize what we're doing?" I asked. "Or it literally can't happen, so I'm crazy for even wasting my time with it?"

"Um, both," he answered. "This is tough to explain. You see, you're fully capable of developing feelings for him."

Okay, I wasn't expecting *that*.

"You just can't act on them."

"Because it would jeopardize the plan," I said, before rolling my eyes. I sighed. This sucked, but I guess I got it. There was a bigger picture to consider here.

"No," he said, catching me by surprise. "I mean you physically can't act upon it. God won't allow it. You have to remember that the main reason He designed you this way was to procreate."

I was confused.

"To reproduce," he added.

I shook my head, agitated.

"*I know what procreate means*," I snapped.

He called me on it. "There's no need for that tone."

"Sorry," I apologized, lowering my head a little. "What you're saying makes sense… unfortunately. Like everything else, though, it'll probably take some getting used to."

"Apology accepted," he continued, with a warm smile.

"I just want you to remember this going forward, and hopefully it will quell any feelings you'll have toward him."

This was his last piece of advice for me that night. After he left, I collapsed on the bed, emotionally drained.

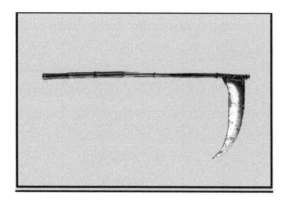

Chapter 10
Shawn

I was awakened by a frantic knock on the door later on that night. I was so tired I didn't even check who was there before I opened it, which was stupid since I had a whole new range of things to concern myself with now.

It was Michelle. She was bruised, battered, and sorry-looking, like she'd been in *another* rumble that night.

I let her in, and held the door open for any more wounded Destinas. She was the only one, though; she was it.

"You're the only one?" I asked, without making eye contact with her yet. I was still checking the front yard out when I asked.

I closed the door and spun around to find a horrid-looking face fully exposed in the well-lit hallway staring back at me.

"*Oh my God*!" I blurted out. Tact was never my strong suit. "Who did this to you?"

She was embarrassed to say, I could tell.

"Michelle?" I asked, pressing her for an answer. "Did the Destinas do this?"

She nodded.

"What happened?" I asked. I was so shocked over this turn of events that I'd forgotten all about what they had shared with me earlier regarding their little initiation ritual and whatnot.

"I got myself jumped out," she admitted.

She pressed a couple of her fingers to the cut just above her left eye, and then brought her hand back down to examine the tips. "*Buena*."

She didn't wipe her hand on her pants or anything at this time, so the bleeding must have stopped.

"Really?" I asked, dumbfounded for sure, but impressed, nonetheless. "Do you mind if I ask why?"

"Well, it all has to do with what you said earlier," she answered. "You know, the Nazareth thing. The whole ride back to the crib I was thinking about that."

I pulled her in for a hug. It just felt like the right thing to do. I mean, who knows what type of beating the poor thing had just taken for us?

She was difficult to look at, that was for sure. It might have been easier to digest if I hadn't already been acquainted with her. When last I saw her, she still had something of a baby face. Whatever they did to her aged her a few years.

The longer I looked, the more used to it I got. This also gave me the opportunity to notice something completely out of place on her face: lipstick.

"Did somebody actually *kiss* you?" I asked. Then, I realized how this may have sounded. "*No*. What I mean is…"

"I knew what you meant," she said, trying to smile. I could tell even this hurt. "It's Kiki's lipstick."

She licked a few fingertips and tried to wipe the lipstick from her face. She was only partially successful, smudging it more than anything.

"Here, let me get it," Lil' Marie said, stepping out from the shadows in the hallway. I didn't even know she was down there with us.

"Sorry, girl," Michelle said, as Lil' Marie wiped the remainder of the lipstick away with a tissue.

"It's whatever, girl," was all Lil' Marie said as she caressed the side of Michelle's bruised face; she was careful around the cuts.

"Come into the bathroom," she added. "We'll get you cleaned up, and figure things out from here."

They probably weren't in there two minutes before one of them broke into tears. Normally, I wouldn't have gone right in there, but I sort of felt like I needed to be part of everything going on.

I realize this sounds beyond self-centered, but I really wasn't myself anymore; I was this new person who served a much greater purpose than he did even a week before. I'm not quite sure how to explain it.

Anyways, Michelle was staring at herself in a mirror for the first time since they jumped her out. As difficult as it was for me to catch that first glimpse of her, I'm sure it hit her tenfold.

Lil' Marie was having a difficult time calming her down.

"Mind if I give it a shot?" I asked, stepping into the bathroom.

"Go for it," Lil' Marie said, with a shrug. Then she stepped aside.

I placed a hand on each of Michelle's shoulders, sort of like a father (or even a mother) would, and then we both stared at her face in the mirror.

"It's probably a lot to take in," I said. "I get that."

"I'm *fea*," she said.

Lil' Marie shook her head. I looked to her, confused. She mouthed the word "ugly."

I nodded my gratitude and locked eyes with Michelle's reflection, once again.

"You are not ugly," I said.

"Are you kidding me?" she asked, with tears still forming. "*Look at me.*"

"Who do you want to impress more than anybody right now?" I asked.

"God and Jesus, I guess. I don't know."

She did know, but this was obviously still a little too fresh to paint a clearer picture for herself.

"Right," I agreed. "Well, they only care about what you can't see in this mirror. They seek *inner beauty*."

She smiled, but it was a nervous one. She wasn't quite ready to dismiss her outward appearance. I could tell just by the way she scrutinized every inch of her face; she was taking into account every bruise and cut, and probably picturing the lasting scars.

"You think so?" she asked, focusing on the largest of her cuts.

I suddenly began quoting one of the passages I read a few nights earlier. It was in Philippians 4. Honestly, I still can't believe I recalled it word for word. Somebody might have been helping me to remember, but I'll never know for sure.

"Finally, brethren, whatever is true, whatever is honorable, whatever is right, whatever is pure, whatever is lovely, whatever is of good repute, if there is any excellence and if anything worthy of praise, let your mind dwell on these things."

She finally looked away from herself and stared into my eyes.

"Thanks for that," she said, through what remained of her tears.

"It's why I'm here."

I almost teared up myself. I didn't, though. Almost doesn't count.

"No," she disagreed. "It's why *I'm* here."

I smiled.

"So, what do we do now?" she asked. "Is there like an oath I need to take or something?"

"No," I laughed. "And I won't be jumping you in either."

"Too soon," she said with a grin.

"Sorry," I apologized. "I do that a lot, by the way."

"What?" she asked. "Stick your foot in your mouth?"

136

"Yeah," I said. "Well, that and I find myself apologizing a lot. I'm not too used to having to be socially acceptable. Until all of this started, it was mostly just my grandfather and me.

I even started complaining about things I probably shouldn't have been complaining about for at least another fifty years or so thanks to him. Stuff like prices. Don't get me wrong. He wasn't a curmudgeon or anything. He was pretty much just your typical old man."

"You miss him," she pointed out. "I can tell."

"Well, yeah." I nodded.

"So, what do you think *he* would think of all of this?" she continued.

"*Him*?" I asked with a smirk of my own. "Well, even though *I* feel like I might be in a little over my head, he'd probably say otherwise. For some reason, that guy was under the impression that I could handle just about anything."

"Well, I mean, I'd say he had good reason to," she said. "You've been through a lot for a suburban white kid."

I laughed. I kind of liked that she didn't pull any punches. I'm very comfortable around people like that.

"You know you can't let him down, right?" she asked. "If he thought you could handle just about anything life threw at you, then I guess now is as good a time as any to prove him right. So, that being said, what's your plan of attack?"

"To get the rest of the Destinas on board, I guess," I answered.

Her eyes widened. I was hoping they wouldn't.

"*Ay Dios mio*. You aim high, don't you?"

"I have to," I said with a shrug. "The sky isn't the limit on this one."

"Who are you gonna go after first?" she asked. I hated how she made this sound somehow malicious because it obviously wasn't. Still, it wasn't a bad idea to develop some sort of a plan of attack.

And, if manipulation had to play a hand in it, then so be it, I guess.

"Who is Kiki's right hand?" I asked.

137

"Rosa, I guess," she answered.

"Well, considering this was all just dropped into her lap, Kiki will probably want all the advice she can get. Am I right?"

Michelle slowly shook her head. I began to do the same.

"Not Kiki," she said. "No. She doesn't really trust anybody enough with the decision-making part of it all. It's just how she is."

Well, so much for *that* plan.

"Why?" she continued, totally catching me by surprise. It seemed like she too could suddenly read my mind, which didn't make any sense since she wasn't any more of an angel than I was.

I took advantage of her question. It was definitely a teachable moment, and I needed all of the practice I could get.

"Well, it seems to me like a lot of frustration comes from giving *and* receiving advice. A lot of times, we second guess the advice we receive, and sometimes we even second guess the advice we give.

"This is good, though, because the way I figure it, we pretty much limit what God can do for us if we think we have all of the answers. Sometimes, we need to just be patient and let *Him* advise us. He wants to give us advice. And the best part is He doesn't need our advice."

"So then, we're getting something for nothing?" she asked. "Right?"

"No," I corrected her. "Your faith and belief in Him is what you're giving Him."

"Okay then, here's my second question: how do we get His advice?" Reasonable question.

"Praying. And it doesn't always need to be 'please bless me or my loved ones with this,' or 'thank you for blessing us with that.' You can just as easily ask Him for advice with something, and I'm telling you He *will* answer you in some fashion. And it's awesome when it happens. *It really is.*"

I let her get acclimated the rest of the night. Then, the next day, I headed out a little early to the bookstore.

I figured I'd need more Bibles for what I had in mind.

When I got back, both Destinas (well, the current and former, I suppose) were in the downstairs bathroom. They looked as though they were getting ready for a night out. *Strange*, I thought.

"What's going on?" I asked. "You girls aren't going out, are you?"

"No," they said in unison.

"Don't worry, *Dad*," Lil' Marie added, rolling her eyes.

Speaking of her eyes, the way she did her make-up, they almost took on an Asian look. And her eyebrows looked even weirder. They looked overly thin and poorly drawn. Michelle's were done up the same way.

"What did you girls do to your faces?" I asked, just barely suppressing my laughter.

They both halted in their application and lowered their arms, mascara, or whatever it was, still in hand. They each shot me something that was probably an angry glare; I couldn't tell for sure what with all of the stuff they had going on around the eyes.

"What?" I continued. "I don't get it."

"This is how we do our faces," Michelle said, waving her hand in a circular motion before her face, with her eyes still fixed on me.

I strode over and picked up one of their eye liner brushes or whatever they're called.

"Come on," I said. "You two must really be bored."

This was a foolish assumption. I had unwittingly mocked a seemingly important ritual of theirs. They looked pissed now.

"Um, it's sort of a big part of who they are, Shawn." Angela spoke from somewhere behind me. "It's the chola look."

"The *chola* look?" I asked.

Suddenly, Lil' Marie and Michelle both pulled a one-eighty to face me. I think they were surprised to hear that word come out of *my* mouth.

139

Lil' Marie must have been too preoccupied to hear Angela. Otherwise, she probably wouldn't have seemed as shocked.

"What do *you* know about the chola look?" Michelle asked, and if I'm not mistaken, she had a little gleam in her eye.

"Nothing," I slowly answered. "It just looked a little…"

"A little *what*?" she continued. They both took on a sort of power stance now. You know, hand on the hip and whatnot. It was a funny one, though, because I could tell they weren't *really* angry with me.

I foolishly played along. It wasn't one of my wiser decisions.

"Clownish," I answered, sporting a half-smile.

They looked to one another, and then back at me. They really did look like different girls, now. Their hair was done up differently, too, sort of 1940s style, if I had to guess.

Honestly, I could only tell it was Michelle under there because of her bruises. *Oh, man.* Now I felt kind of bad. If this was a huge part of who they were, maybe this was Michelle trying to feel normal again instead of having to look at her battered face.

"Clownish, huh?" Lil' Marie asked.

She playfully bit down on her bottom lip, and arched one of her eyebrows. I got the sense I was in for it.

Michelle chuckled; I could tell she was going to enjoy whatever was coming to me.

They stepped to me, make-up in hand. I instinctively backed away from the bathroom doorway, thinking they were only interested in chasing me from the room like I was some annoying little brother, so they could get back to "doing" their faces; another foolish assumption on my part.

I didn't take my eyes off of them. I wish I would have. If I had, perhaps I would have seen the ottoman in my path. I didn't though, and as a result, found myself on my keister on the living room floor.

They just stood over me for a minute, grinning away. Lil' Marie extended her right hand, which I foolishly took for a sign of hospitality.

It was nothing more than a trap, of course. She tricked me into the mindset that I was being helped to my feet, so I'd let my defenses down, I guess.

Then she forced me onto my back and mounted my chest. It was too unexpected to turn me on, which I suppose was a good thing in hindsight. She was a little heavier than you would have thought, too, especially with a name like *Lil'* Marie.

"Okay, okay," I said, panting for the most part. "Fun's over. Off of me."

"Not yet," she said, panting a little herself. Hers must have been a little more relaxed, though, if that makes any sense. I only think this because she was holding on to that grin.

I started to grin, now, which luckily confused her. She wasn't the only one who could play someone.

"What are *you* grinning about?" she asked.

"Yeah?" added Michelle. "What's so funny, white boy?"

I know this sounds weird, but I was starting to get a kick out of them calling me "white boy." Was it racist? Maybe. Who knows? I mean, *I* didn't really consider it too racist.

"Nothing. It's just that I've always sort of had a thing for Asian girls."

Man, I was barely able to withhold my laughter when I said this last bit.

"*Oh, really?*" Lil' Marie asked, faking fuming. "Well, let's see how you like *this*."

She suddenly skooched forward so her knees were now completely pinning my arms down, shoulders and all.

"Quick, Michelle, gimme the eyebrow pencil," she said. "We're gonna chola him up."

"*Wait!*" I said. "*What?*"

They shared a laugh, and it was one of those laughs you wanted to be in on, not the other way around.

141

"We'll need more than the eyebrow pencil then," Michelle joked. Only I'm afraid it wasn't actually a joke.

I tried to force my way out from under Lil' Marie's weight, but the only part of my upper torso I could move was pretty much my head. And Michelle, as expected, put an end to even that much when she held it straight with one hand on each side. I locked eyes with her. She was excited, enjoying every minute of this.

Lil' Marie, in the meantime, brought the pencil down to my forehead. The funny thing was it looked a lot like a regular old colored pencil. I felt her draw a second set of eyebrows just above my own. She burst into laughter once she was finished and got a good look at her work, as did Michelle.

"Aight, aight," I said, mocking them a little; I'm not sure what I was thinking doing that. "Now let me up, so I can go wash this stuff off."

"Sorry," said Lil' Marie, only she obviously didn't mean it. "You wanted to act like a pesky little brother. Well, this is what I used to do to my brother whenever *he* wouldn't leave us alone."

"*No!*" I shouted. It wasn't because of what she said, it was because of what I saw her do: unscrew her mascara brush.

"Hey, this is what you get for calling a Destina an Asian girl," she joked.

"That *was* mad disrespectful," Michelle added.

"But I didn't know," I said, half-smiling, which in no way helped my case.

The instant the mascara brush touched my face, I forced my way out from under her. She fell to the right, which I felt sort of sorry about. But, hey, all's fair in sissification and war.

And besides, it wasn't like I actually hit her or even pushed her for that matter. All I did was scramble out from under her, and make a mad dash for the bathroom to wipe my new eyebrows off with a damp facecloth.

Why, I didn't even waste a second checking them out in the mirror. Out of sight, out of mind.

My forehead reddened over from all of the scrubbing. Even though there weren't any other guys around, I scrubbed like there was a whole frat house full of guys out there.

Angela stepped into the room, and immediately burst into laughter. I simply shook my head; what else could I do?

"They needed this, you know," she said. "So, thanks."

"Anytime," I said, sporting a half-smile.

"So, what are your thoughts on Lil' Marie?" she asked.

I hesitated. I really didn't know what she was asking. Was she asking if I was attracted to her, or was she asking me something else?

"Meaning?" I asked, as I grabbed the hand towel from the rack to dry my forehead. Now *she* looked a little confused.

"Her *faith*," she said.

I think she might have overdone it a little, though, because she didn't come across as nonchalant as I think she intended to. She didn't respond to this observation of mine, so who knows what was up with her?

"Do you think she's changed any since that nonsense in the car?" she added.

"I doubt it," I answered. "At least, I don't *think* she has. Can't you just read her thoughts on this, so we know for sure?"

She shook her head, and I furrowed my eyebrows as a result. I took it for Michael butting in, again.

"That's not it. I've tried, but she hasn't really been thinking about her faith all that much. Which could mean one of two things.

"Either she has no faith and the whole idea to her is barely worth a thought, or she's never honestly lost her faith and she was just trying to get a rise out of us.

"Whatever the case may be, she hasn't been questioning her faith. I'd have known about it."

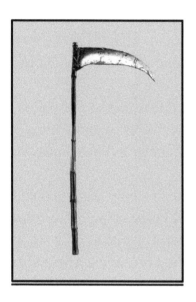

<u>**Chapter 11**</u>
Angela

I had a lot on my mind that night, so much so that if I did get tired anymore, I probably would have been exhausted the next morning due to a lack of sleep. Shawn was doing great so far, but I could tell he felt a little in over his head.

This was to be expected, though. I mean, he did have a manual to go by – the ultimate manual, really, but it wasn't like they made a teacher's edition.

For whatever reason (a.k.a. divine intervention), I went outside to clear my head. Looking up at the stars has always helped me with that. I'm not even that into astronomy.

145

I guess it's just the easiest way to get my mind off of more pressing things – like battling Satan's forces for example.

It turns out, though, that I'd have been better off inside. You see, while my mind was thousands of miles above me, the rest of me was a sitting duck for one of Satan's angels. I should have figured it wouldn't take them long to track us down.

He snuck right up on me and sort of pulled me into an awkward choke hold. Unfortunately, it was so unorthodox it took me nearly a minute to figure out just how to counter it. I hate inexperienced fighters. How ironic is that?

The way he had me, the only thing I could do to break the hold was reach up, grab the back of his head, pull it forward so his chin was resting on top of my head, and quickly drop to my butt, while still holding on.

This sent him reeling off somewhere and he collapsed shortly thereafter. He was only slightly moving around, sprawled out face-down on the ground.

For some reason, I drew a blank on what to do. I took a step back – on instinct more than anything, I guess – and stumbled over the answer to my dilemma. I reached down and picked up a rock my former self most likely could have only shifted around a little, and then brought it down on the back of his head.

Needless to say, he stopped moving. *What had become of me?*

As if on cue, Michael stepped out from the shadows. Did all of his entrances need to be mysterious? Talk about having a flair for the dramatic.

"I'm a little too concerned to be entertained by your observation, young lady," he said.

I couldn't help but feel a little ashamed.

"It's nothing to be *ashamed* of," he continued.

"You're worried that you've become some sort of a killer. This is a normal enough reaction. There are a few things you need to remember, though. For starters, these have all been acts of self-defense. Believe me, they'll stop at nothing to kill you.

"And on top of saving yourself, you're helping to save the Kingdom of Heaven. Then there's the fact that these aren't actually human beings you're killing. They may look it, but they're closer to demons. Finally, *He* wants you to do this, which should be enough. Don't you think?"

I nodded. He was right.

"Good girl," he said with a wink.

His eyes didn't match his smile, though.

"Look," he continued. "I know this is difficult for you. Just know that you aren't doing anything wrong."

"I know," I said.

Then, as mysteriously as he had arrived, he was gone. I expected nothing less.

I went back inside and thought about my latest kill for the next hour or so. Who was he there for? It couldn't have been Michelle because *she* had chosen Jesus over the Destinas. So then, it was Lil' Marie?

I knew she was a pain in the butt a few days earlier, but she had for the most part given that anti-God business a rest and I didn't think she'd killed anyone or anything like that.

After breakfast, Shawn asked us to join him in the living room. He had something to say to the girls.

"I was reading Philippians last night and I thought of you girls right away. Well, mostly you, Lil' Marie," he said.

"I only planned on reading some of it, but it's such a short read that I ended up finishing it all. It's a letter from Paul to Christ's other followers. In it, he says…"

He was interrupted by a knock at the front door. He looked toward the doorway, confused, and then back at the girls – and me.

"Kiki and the others, you think?" he asked.

Michelle shrugged, and Lil' Marie assumed the *Destinos,* of all people. What would *they* be doing here?

From where I sat, I could only see Shawn standing in the doorway. I still couldn't see any of them yet. Perhaps they were patiently waiting for him to invite them in. He was stunned, speechless.

"Well, aren't you gonna invite us in?" one of them asked. Turns out it was the Destinos.

He figured they'd be coming in regardless, so he nodded – still speechless, though.

"*Gracias,*" said the first one to enter. He, plus the four he had with him, joined us.

Shawn reluctantly followed them in. The poor thing had no idea what was going on. I didn't either, but I didn't really get intimidated in their presence anymore.

I used to back when they'd ride up on me and Lucia if we were hanging out somewhere. A few of them could be classified as cute, I guess, but I wasn't for that life, so I forced myself not to be interested, which wasn't always the easiest thing to do.

"Nice crib, bro," said Luis, the guy who always seemed like their leader to me.

"Thanks," Shawn replied, still very nervous.

I snuck a look at Lil' Marie, who was grinning away. This was obviously a set-up. Michelle, naturally, looked pretty uneasy herself. They all gave her an unimpressed look on their way into the living room; I guess this was to be expected.

"Nice shiner, girl," Luis said to Michelle, rather coldly. I didn't like that.

"And you guys are?" Shawn asked, feeling a little nervous right after he blurted it out. He was afraid it made him sound like some sort of a wise-ass. I think that's just a white boy thing.

"The Destinos," I said, beneath my breath.

"*The Destinos?*" he quickly asked. "There are Destin*os?*"

"Yeah, bro," Luis answered, even though the question wasn't necessarily directed at him.

"Don't disrespect," said another of the Destinos, getting a little heated.

Shawn began shaking his head, with his mouth open.

"Chill, *vato*," Luis interrupted, signaling for his man to settle down.

He then re-directed his attention to a nearly trembling Shawn.

"Relax," he suggested, placing his hand on Shawn's shoulder. Anyone could tell Shawn was still nervous as all get-out because his shoulder sort of dropped the instant Luis put any kind of pressure on it.

"Ramon just gets a little heated sometimes. He's not gonna do anything to you; none of us are. In fact, we wanna thank you for letting Lil' Marie stay here. Good looks, bro. *Gracias*."

It's safe to say I was as surprised as Shawn was when Luis pulled him in for a hug, complete with a pat to the back. I couldn't tell how genuine it was, but at least it was something.

"I mean, I don't know what *she's* doing here, too," he continued. He was referring to Michelle. "But, hey, that's your business, not mine anymore. So, it's whatever. Good riddance."

Shawn wanted to defend Michelle's honor, but he held his tongue. This might have been a wise choice for the time being. Still, she looked a little hurt that he didn't.

The Destinos all took seats on the sofa; the girls moved for them.

"We didn't mean to disrupt whatever you had going on," Luis said.

"Please, continue."

"Um, okay," Shawn said.

Then, he picked his Bible up from the coffee table and set about reading from Philippians 3. He looked a little shaken as he read. They had definitely gotten to him whether it was their intention or not. To his credit, though, he pressed on.

"Dear brothers and sisters, pattern your lives after mine and learn from those who follow our example. For I have told you often before, and I say it again with tears in my eyes, that there are many whose conduct shows they are really enemies of the cross of Christ. They are headed for destruction. Their god is their appetite, they brag about shameful things, and they think only about this life here on earth."

A couple of Destinos snickered. To his credit, Luis flashed them a disapproving glance. They offered him a confused shrug.

"Is that for us?" he asked.

"It's for all of us," Shawn replied.

"Well, what else does it say?"

Shawn was a little more comfortable with his next piece of Biblical advice.

"Fix your thoughts on what is true, and honorable, and right, and pure, and lovely, and admirable. Think about things that are excelled and worthy of praise."

The Destinos pretty much all stood up at once. Surprisingly, Shawn didn't take a step back. I thought for sure there would have been at least a little cowering on his part. Not the case, though.

"Okay, bro," began Luis. "Well, we've got somewhere to be, so we're gonna dip. We'll see each other soon, though."

Shawn nodded. He didn't have much choice in the matter; they knew where he lived now. *How* did they, though? There was the million-dollar question. My guess was Kiki had told them. Once they were gone, Shawn addressed us.

"Well, hey," he began, surprisingly chipper now. "At least they stuck around for the Word."

"Yeah," Lil' Marie said with a smirk. "But do you really think you've made any kind of an impact on them?"

"If you have faith as small as a mustard seed," Shawn began. Hmm, impressive. He now had Matthew co-signing for him. "Then you can move a mountain."

Lil' Marie rolled her eyes.

"Whatever that means."

"Stop selling 'em, girl," Michelle said. "You know what he's saying."

"Yeah, I know," she confessed.

"Listen, all this mustard seed talk's gettin' me hungry," Michelle continued. "I'm starving like a homeless person."

A light bulb went off in Shawn's head when he heard this. *A soup kitchen.* They could help feed the homeless. This would boost their image around the neighborhood.

He figured this was just the type of PR move that could make them look good. Could he sell them on it, though? I wasn't altogether sure they had it in them. Time would tell, though, and hopefully prove me wrong.

I had a place in mind for where they could do this. It was called Marie's Place. Mama and I used to volunteer there every other Saturday for a few hours. It was like a cafeteria in this big, brick building. I'm not sure what else they had there. All I ever saw was the cafeteria and occasionally the kitchen.

My job, for the most part, was to just pass food out at the tables and collect the bowls and anything else when the people were done eating. At first, it got to be a little disgusting, but I got used to it after a while.

When you get it in your head that you're doing something nice for someone who really needs it, then it isn't *so* bad when you accidentally dip your thumb in their left-over minestrone soup.

"There's a great one called Marie's Place back in our neighborhood," I informed him.

Lil' Marie shot me a quick, confused glance.

"Marie's Place?" she asked. "What does *that* place have to do with anything?"

Oh boy. Her tone alone suggested she wouldn't be game for it. This would take some convincing, I could tell.

"We're looking to boost your image," Shawn said. "Remember when we talked about Nazareth?"

"Yeah," she recalled. "I know we – well, *you* – talked about it, but I never actually agreed to anything."

"Is this all you want out of life?" he asked her, point-blank. "Is *this* going to be your legacy? Street fights and hiding from the *boys*?"

"Look, Shawn, people like me don't have a 'legacy.' We never have, and we never will. That's something white people worry about, not us."

Shawn rolled his eyes. He knew a cop-out when he heard one.

"You know, a man wiser than me once said, 'Past judgments will bind you if you let them.' In other words, *you're* doing this to yourself now. You have an opportunity to turn this around if you want to. Now if you don't take it, then I don't want to hear you pissing and moaning about getting suspicious looks from store clerks or anything like that. Feel me?"

"You got that," she replied. "I'll take that short."

"That wasn't a *short*, Lil' Marie," Michelle chimed in, clearly annoyed.

It was a relief to not be able to read one of their minds for a change. This meant she wasn't going anywhere anytime soon. At least, I think this was what it meant.

"It's whatever," Lil' Marie came back with, as though she were above all of this. "Say no more."

With that, she shook her head and left the room, once again playing the fake sense of maturity card. Definitely a gang-banger tactic; well, it was one I'd seen enough.

Shawn left the room as well. He mentioned something about having work to do. The work he was referring to was that of locating the contact information for Marie's Place and ultimately pinning down a day for them to help out, which wasn't too difficult since they pretty much needed whatever help they could get whenever they could get it.

A couple of hours later, there was a knock at the front door. Kiki had come back, alone. She had a laundry bag at her feet, which surprised us all.

"What, do you want me to do your laundry now, too?" Shawn joked.

Judging by her expression, she wasn't in a joking mood.

"Now's not the time, okay?" she said.

He awkwardly corrected his smile.

"Sorry," he apologized, taking a step back. "What's up?"

"We lost the house," she said. "They took it."

She didn't look too angry over it. In fact, she looked more morose than anything, leading me to assume she knew it was coming.

"Where's your mom?" Michelle asked.

Then her eyes widened.

"Oh, sorry," she quickly added, falling back a little. I'm sure it was easy to forget she was no longer a Destina.

"*No*," Kiki said, with sympathetic eyes. "It ain't like that; you're still my girl. I don't know where Mama is. That's part of the problem. A big part, in fact. She hasn't been paying for the house. They said she missed a few payments. Not just one or two. They said she left them no choice."

"Yeah," Lil' Marie sneered. "I bet if you were white…"

Shawn was suddenly really uncomfortable.

"Don't do that, girl," Kiki said. "Can't play the race card here. It is what it is."

Lil' Marie fell back.

"Man, this was the last thing I needed," Kiki continued. "What with this whole Lucia mess."

"What's happening with that?" Shawn asked, a little softly and cautiously.

"The boys have been asking around, but nobody's saying nothing," she answered, glancing back at Shawn's neighbors across the way, clearly agitated.

Shawn was about to correct her grammar, but he fortunately thought better of it.

"It's funny," Kiki continued. "It feels weird when people won't snitch when it's one of *yours* that got bodied. Plus, the boys' job just got a little easier, so I doubt they'll dig too deep for answers. She's just another dead gang-banger. What do they care? It's whatever, though."

She shrugged.

"So, do you have room for me in there?" she asked, motioning inside.

Shawn bent over and awkwardly scooped her laundry bag up into his arms in such a fashion that it looked as though some of her clothes might spill out. She looked a little too concerned, leading me to believe she was bringing more than just clothes into the house.

"Sure, we do," he said, before spinning around and climbing the stairs.

I wanted to follow him upstairs to see if I was right about her bag, but I didn't want to always be holding his hand. He was older than me for crying out loud.

The only thing I could do, which I did end up doing, was check her waist area for a bulge. Sure enough, there was one there shaped very much like the barrel of a nine.

I was hoping Shawn wouldn't make an issue of it – even though he would have every right to – because she'd have probably left *us* instead of ditching her piece.

By the time he got back downstairs, we were all huddled around the dining room table, playing Spades. Well, *they* were playing; I was watching. Every now and then, Lil' Marie would look to me, expecting me to throw a card down. The first few times, she chuckled at herself under her breath, and shook it off.

"You have good taste in beer for a white boy," Kiki said, raising a bottle of light beer. "I hope you don't mind."

She then took another hearty swig. He offered her a weird look.

"No," he replied. "It's actually not even mine. It was my grandfather's."

She immediately spit the remaining beer from her mouth, spraying the pile of cards.

"Well, I guess that's game," joked Lil' Marie.

"I drank a *dead* guy's beer?" Kiki asked, incredulously.

"Even worse, I'm afraid," added Shawn. "A dead guy who hasn't lived here in a *long* time. I guess you should have checked the born-on date."

He grinned.

"Ha, ha, ha," she began, sarcastically. "Very funny."

She then flung one of her cards through the air in his direction. It curved around him, nearly catching him in the ear. He dodged it a little after the fact. Horrible reflexes; he'd never be able to fend off one of Satan's angels.

"Oh, by the way, everyone," he began. "I've scheduled us a date to volunteer at Marie's Place. Now, I can't force you to volunteer, but I'll be doing it and I hope I won't be alone. *Kiki*, are you up for something like this?"

"Sorry, man," she apologized. "But I've already found my homeless shelter."

She slapped the tabletop with her right palm.

He looked a little down.

"Hey, I'm just messing with you," she said. "I mean, I'm probably not gonna volunteer this time around, but you never know about the next time. Good enough?"

"Yeah," he answered, nodding. He'd take it.

He looked to the others for some sort of response. Lil' Marie had no interest in it whatsoever, but she didn't come right out and say it.

It was just after dinner when we saw a set of headlights soar across the living room ceiling; somebody was pulling into the driveway. It was Luis and a carload of Destinos.

Surprisingly, I couldn't hear their bass pumping. I take it they were respecting the neighbors. I didn't know they cared.

As they made their way through the front door, I noticed a dude I'd never seen chilling with them before. He didn't notice me, though, so I guessed there was no real cause for alarm. I have to admit it, I was getting pretty antsy lately. Sometimes, I wish angels didn't look like everyone else.

"Bro!" Luis shouted, to get Shawn's attention, I guess; I didn't deem this measure necessary. "How come you didn't tell us you were dying?"

"*What?*" he asked, panicking. "Who told you?"

"Does it matter?" Luis asked, quickly glancing in Lil' Marie's direction. Shawn didn't catch it, but I sure did, so I shot her a glare. She pretended not to notice. "All that matters is you need to get busy living like there's no tomorrow. Feel me, fam?"

"*Fam?*" Shawn asked.

He would have fought Luis on this "fam" business, but he was too disappointed in whoever had betrayed him. He still hadn't pieced together that it was Lil' Marie.

"We'll hit up the liquor store we passed on our way here," Luis announced. "We gonna treat tonight like it's your bachelor party, bro."

The other Destinos all nodded in agreement, with ear-to-ear grins.

"No," Shawn quickly said, shaking his head. "No, thanks. I'm good."

"*Whatchu mean?* We gonna turn it up tonight. And I'm not talkin' about white boy partying either. We gonna show you how *we* do."

Upon saying this, he slammed his right fist against his chest like he had just knocked down a three in somebody's face.

156

Shawn was uncomfortable now, as was I. He was no longer angry over being betrayed. He was already picturing *who knows what* kind of drugs, drunk gangstas, nines going off, neighbors' lights going on, and finally, the boys showing up.

Was this how he wanted to be remembered? As a pain in the butt disturber of the peace? He used a less family-friendly word than "butt;" that's how I knew he was panicky.

"Look, bro," Luis continued, in a much calmer tone. He draped his arm across Shawn's shoulders and escorted him off toward the dining room. Clearly, whatever he had to say wasn't meant for everyone's ears. I followed them in, though; there was nothing he could do about it.

Once we were in there, he continued.

"We're not gonna get you into any trouble if that's what you're worried about. For starters, why would we risk getting into any trouble ourselves? We're not stupid. We know the boys are a lot quicker to show up to a crib out here than they are back in our hood. Secondly, you're doing us a solid by letting the shorties stay here. Why would I disrespect you like that?"

"I don't know," answered Shawn. "You wouldn't, I guess."

Luis shook his head.

"So, we're good?"

"No drugs or guns, right?" Shawn blurted out.

"*Bro*?" Luis said, taking a step backward, with his arms open, pretending to be offended. At least he looked like he was faking it.

"Just a few drinks, I swear," he added. "And we're all adults, so you've got nothing to worry about there."

I think Shawn noticed me shaking my head, but he chose to ignore my wishes anyways.

"What the hell," he said, with a shrug.

"Perfect," Luis said. "I'll have one of my boys run up the street to grab whatever we're drinking. What do you usually get wavy on? It's on us."

He gave Shawn a gentle tap on the cheek, sort of like they sometimes do in mob movies. Danger! Danger! Shawn was beginning to feel like he belonged – like he was cool. This was exactly what I was worried about.

"We're gonna treat you to something else, too," he added, with a devilish gleam in his eye. "The rest of the Destinas are on their way over."

"Okay," Shawn said, a little absentmindedly. He didn't catch on immediately. He was too concerned with a house party ensuing.

Luis snapped his fingers in Shawn's face.

"You with me, bro? I'm saying you can have your pick tonight. Any one of our shorties you want."

"*Your* shorties?" Shawn asked, incredulously.

"Yeah," Luis answered, pulling rank. "Just because they're under your roof…"

Shawn quickly grew nervous.

"Oh, that's not what I'm…"

Luis burst into laughter.

"I know," he laughed, reassuring him. "I'm just messing with you. Yeah, you definitely need to get a little wavy tonight."

Wow! You couldn't sleep on Luis. That's for sure. I bet he could talk anybody into just about anything.

Shawn finally bit the bullet and glanced over at me. He figured his little charade had gone on long enough. I neither shook my head nor said a disparaging word. He was a grown man, who didn't have much longer to live. Therefore, I left this one up to him.

He faced Luis once again, with a dejected look in his eyes.

"I'm sorry, man," he apologized. "I just don't think it would be very fair to the girl. I mean, I *am* dying."

"Bro, they *know* that," Luis pointed out. "Don't worry. It's not like any of them are looking for anything serious anyways. They're all spoken for. Well, all except for Michelle, but I'm pretty sure she'll still do whatever we say."

"Really?" Shawn asked, a little disgruntled now, and who could blame him?

"Yeah," Luis confirmed. "It's like *Timothy* said: 'Let a woman learn quietly with all submissiveness. I do not permit a woman to teach or exercise authority over man.' Oh, no offense, by the way. From what I understand, you're answering to a female these days."

Shawn was taken aback, as was I, and rightly so. I did *not* see this coming.

"Did you get that Timothy stuff out of the Bible?" he asked, purposely avoiding discussing me.

Luis's eyes instantly lit up.

"Don't tell me *I* just quoted unfamiliar scripture to the *preacher*."

Shawn grew embarrassed.

"First of all, I'm not actually a…" Shawn began, before quickly being interrupted.

"Bro, relax, I'm just pushing your buttons. You know, to let you know you're not the only one who knows the Bible around here. I read it cover to cover a couple of times when I was locked up. It's pretty much all I did in there. Well, that and lift weights. It was the only way I could stay out of trouble and get out on time."

"Wow!" Shawn said. "I had no idea."

"What?" Luis asked, incredulously. "That I was locked up?"

"No," Shawn answered. "That's not surprising. I'm more…"

"*Really*?" Luis asked, pretending to take offense.

Shawn pathetically raised his hands to sort of shield himself.

"I meant about the Bible," he blurted out.

Luis began chuckling.

"You're too easy. But, hey, 'the meek shall inherit the earth,' right?"

Shawn mulled this one over and then hung his head low.

"Oh, right," Luis continued. "I guess this isn't really the case for you. Don't worry, bro. I'm sure a good white boy like you is headed to Heaven."

Shawn chuckled under his breath.

"What's so funny?" Luis asked, sort of grinning.

"Nothing really. It's just kind of weird that you've read the whole thing a couple of times through, and you *still* lead the kind of life you lead. No offense, but…"

All of a sudden, Luis unbuttoned his right shirt cuff and began rolling his sleeve up.

Shawn, in typical fashion, braced himself for some sort of a beat down. He figured he'd gotten away with one earlier, but judging Luis's lifestyle may have been pushing the envelope a little too far.

As it turned out, though, he had nothing to worry about because Luis was only showing him the tattoo he had of the cross on his forearm.

"There are some things we all have in common," he said. "Other than that, we're each a product of our environment."

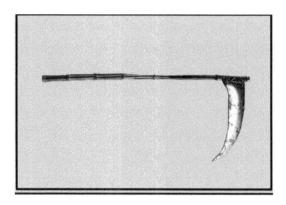

Chapter 12
Shawn

I really couldn't figure this guy out. I mean, he didn't seem *that* bad to me. Wait, let me re-phrase this, so I don't come off as some male-chauvinistic jerk. He didn't seem as bad as I thought a gang leader would be.

While I fully expected him to have very little respect for women, I also pegged him for somebody who would be cursing up a storm and trying his best to look physically intimidating. Neither of these was the case.

He definitely looked the part, but he didn't necessarily act it, not to the full extent, at least. Then again, this was a stereotype I could mostly attribute to gangsta rap videos.

"As strange as it sounds, I've never given my environment much thought," I said. And, I hadn't really, it was true.

161

"That's probably because you've had it easy until now," Luis said.

He obviously hadn't heard much about me. "Your folks are probably great people. My pop's upstate, waiting to hear from the President every year."

"Huh?" I began. "What do you mean?"

"You know how the President pardons a bunch of prisoners each year? Well, my pop keeps hoping he'll make the list. He even prays for it, if you can believe it. He was sure he'd get the call now that we had a brotha in there. Yeah, he isn't Hispanic, but at least he isn't some old white dude. Feel me?"

"Yikes!" I said. "I'm willing to bet the odds of making *that* list are still up there with winning the lottery."

"Probably," Luis said, with a smirk. "That's why I told him he was better off praying for God's pardon instead of the President's. With God, it's a sure thing you'll get pardoned. You don't need to make any list."

"It's true," I agreed.

"I hope so," he added. "It's what keeps me going. I mean, I'd have probably bodied *all* of my enemies by now, if I didn't believe it."

This was certainly a scary thing to say. Was he actually admitting to me that he had killed somebody? Or was he simply saying he'd probably have a total disregard for human life if it weren't for this possible light at the end of the tunnel?

"Let me ask you something," he continued.

I nodded.

"This Angela stuff, is it for real?"

"Yeah," I answered. "Of course it is. I mean, look at me. Do you think I'd be crazy enough to show up in *your* neighborhood, and tell *those* girls that I'd been chilling with their dead friend?"

"Good point," he admitted. "So, what's your plan, then?"

I naturally didn't want to share it with him just yet, but I also didn't want to lie, so I needed to dance around his question, hoping he wouldn't notice.

"Don't know," I said. "To be honest with you, I've sort of been taking my cues here and there from Angela."

He was eyeing me suspiciously now. He actually looked a little hurt if you want to know the truth, which might have had everything to do with the heart to heart we had sort of just had.

"You aren't lying to me, are you?" he asked, with a sigh.

"Because there's probably nothing I can do to Angela anymore, but there's still plenty I can do to you. Just keep that in mind, okay?"

This was the Luis I expected to run into sooner or later.

The rest of the Destinas showed up a short time later, and I'll tell you one thing: they sure as heck weren't dressed like they were the night Lucia died. They had these sexy black little numbers on that even I can admit were kind of on the short side.

They didn't leave much to the imagination.

Each pair of eyes sought me out once they joined us inside, leading me to assume Luis had caught them up to speed on his plans to fix me up that night. They all certainly looked game for it, that was for sure.

Believe it or not, it was about the most uncomfortable I'd ever been, and I had once buried both of my parents on the same day.

The Destinas had barely made eye contact with me the last time we were all together – granted, it was about as crazy a night as I could have ever imagined, which left us with very few opportunities to flirt with one another – and now they were all probably more than willing to have sex with me at Luis's request.

He just stood there, grinning away, glancing back and forth between me and the girls. His boys were grinning, too. I couldn't take my eyes off of the girls after a while, not because I wanted to sleep with them all, but simply because they were all still stunning in spite of the predicament they found themselves in.

The timing couldn't have been worse for this. When I had told Luis earlier that I wasn't interested in having sex with any of them that night, it was more or less a promise to the Lord, too.

"Well, have you changed your mind about what we discussed?" he asked.

I sighed and quickly shook my head.

"*Really*?" he asked. "No offense, bro, but are you sure you even like women?"

The girls each looked to be forcing a frown, probably for Luis's benefit more than anything else. I could tell they didn't want to disappoint him, but at the same time, they were probably thrilled they wouldn't be pressured into having sex anymore.

I wasn't offended; how could I have been? I mean, I would have been just as much to blame as him in all of this. To be honest with you, I just wanted to get out of there and be done with it.

"Actually, I think I'm good with everything anyways," I explained. "I've kind of got a migraine going, so I think I'm just gonna head up to my room for the night. You guys can stay, though. Can you just do me a favor and keep the volume down? I'm gonna try to sleep this off."

"Yeah," he said, confused. "Sure. Get some rest, okay?"

I glanced at Angela on my way upstairs. "The things I do for you," I thought to us both.

"*Gracias*," I heard her say, just before I reached the top step.

Once inside, I looked at my lonely bed, focusing mainly where the mattress dipped on the left side.

That night, I dubbed it Death Valley for obvious reasons. Pathetic.

I was already in my lucky boxers and a tee when I heard a soft knock on the door. Keep in mind, they were only my "lucky" boxers because they had a shamrock pattern, no other reason.

I thought all that was about to change, though, once I heard *that* knock. There was no urgency to it; it seemed like the kind of knock a person went with when they were intent on seducing you, even when they weren't all that interested in you.

I wondered which girl Luis had sent up against my wishes.

I have to be honest. I didn't know what I was going to do this time around since I no longer had an audience and there was no place to retreat to. Retreat to? Pathetic.

What I finally did was I pulled a pair of flannel pants on and tied the drawstring; I figured this'd be a good enough reminder to keep me on the right path. However, I'm pretty sure checking my breath on my way to the door quickly negated any allusions I created with the drawstring.

I opened the door to find nothing but hallway in both directions; so much for luck. It's like Angela always says, though: there's no such thing as luck. Speaking of her, she showed herself in the doorway just as I was closing it.

"*Oh*," I began. "Was that you just now?"

"No," she said, confusedly. "It was probably Lil' Marie and that new dude she was flirting with."

"Which one?" I asked. "I don't remember any of that going on. Not while I was down there, at least."

"He had the white fitted on," she explained. "Now, do you remember him?"

I had no idea who she was talking about. She suddenly grew nervous. I could see it in her eyes; they gradually widened as she pieced something together.

"Nobody had a white hat on down there, Angela," I said.

Suddenly, it must have hit her.

"*Oh, no*!" she shouted, and then bolted down the hallway and into Lil' Marie's bedroom.

We found her kissing the air, which, of course, threw me for a loop. Against my wishes, it seemed as though drugs *had* found their way into my house after all. Damn.

She suddenly fell back onto the bed, with her legs dangling over the side. Whatever she took, it worked quickly.

"*No*!" Angela shouted. "Leave her alone!"

She rushed the bed and threw a punch into the air. As she brought her arm back around, a dude a little bigger than me suddenly appeared falling from the bed; his white hat landed on the floor beside him.

That was the guy! No wonder I didn't see him.

She grabbed a pillow from the bed and covered his face. He struggled beneath her weight.

"*Quick!* Check her for signs of life, Shawn!" she shouted.

"It might not be too late."

"*What's happening*?" I shouted.

She ignored me.

I hurried over and pressed my fingers to Lil' Marie's throat. Nothing. Then I lifted her wrist and tried my luck there.

Again, nothing. I panicked.

After all, I had a murdered girl in my home, her closest friends and fellow gang members were all downstairs, and I couldn't explain a thing to them because they couldn't have seen the dude in the white hat either.

I looked to Angela to see how she was making out on her end. She was better off than me for her problem was already gone – vanished; she was left pressing a pillow into the carpet.

Even his hat was gone; so much for that. I was officially screwed. As if on cue, we heard a bunch of footsteps climbing the stairs. They must have heard me scurrying around up there.

Luis was the first through the door. He looked more confused than anything, which I guess was to be expected since she didn't really look all that dead yet. Angels don't leave any blood.

"We heard a lot of noise up here," he said. "What's going on?"

He glanced over at Lil' Marie sprawled out on the bed.

"What's with her?" he continued.

"She's dead," I admitted. I honestly didn't see the point in playing dumb here.

"*What*?" he asked, losing his temper pretty quickly. This was a side of him I hadn't *really* seen yet. "How?"

166

"You're not gonna believe it, but I'll tell you anyways."

He crossed his arms, waiting. It might have also been because he was getting fidgety; I'm not sure if anyone else noticed.

"I think you let one of Satan's angels in," I explained.

Angela instantly slapped her palm against her forehead. I couldn't help but notice.

"Sorry," I quickly apologized. "Poor choice of words. He came in *with* you guys."

"I thought he was a friend of theirs because he didn't make eye contact with me. He tricked me," she said. "Tell them that."

This sucked. The only other person who could have confirmed Angela's being in the room with us was now dead.

"Angela thought he was with you because he was smart enough not to make eye contact with her. If he had, it would have meant one of two things: that he was either one of the next ones on her list or he was one of Satan's boys – one of his angels."

Luis began shaking his head. He wasn't happy with me.

"What the hell are you talking about?" he finally asked. "*Satan*? Are you serious?"

"It's crazy," I continued. "I know. I felt the same way the first time I met her."

"You're screwed-up in the head," he came back with. "You know that?"

I'm not going to lie. For once, this did occur to me. Now, more than ever, I really needed this Angel of Death thing to be on the up and up. If it wasn't, then I'd either be killed by Luis right then and there or at the very least going away for a long time.

While it's true they would have had nothing but circumstantial evidence to go on, I'm sure this would have been more than enough considering my luck.

Then again, maybe I'd luck out and they, too, would think I was insane.

"No, you're not," Angela quickly pointed out. "Not how you think, at least."

I gave her a look. This wasn't the best time to zing me with a one-liner, no matter how clever.

"Sorry," she apologized. "What I mean is: how could Lil' Marie have seen and heard me, too, if I was only a figment of *your* imagination? Think about it."

She was right. This was a relief, maybe.

"Lil' Marie saw her, too," I quickly said, motioning to the corpse. "But she's dead now, so…"

"You have me at a crossroad," Luis said with a sigh.

"Meaning?" I asked, growing a little nervous.

He lifted his tee up in front to reveal the handle of his gun, tucked into his jeans. I took a couple of steps back, shaking my head the whole time.

"*Dude*, I swear to God I didn't do this!"

"Anybody can say that," he said. "Doesn't make it true."

"*I* can't just say it anymore, I don't think."

Of course, I didn't know for sure, but I was *fairly* certain I couldn't say this anymore unless I truly meant it.

"Put yourself in my shoes," he said, sounding as rational as I'm sure he could have at the time. "One of our shorties is *dead*, and you were the only one up here with her. How does that look?"

"Well, she must have seen him, too," I frantically pointed out. "I mean, why else would she have come up here while there was a party going on – or whatever this is?"

"That doesn't mean anything," he said. "Maybe she was just running up here to grab something, or maybe she got a 'headache' like you."

Damn. He wasted no time in poking holes in my alibi. Leave it to a criminal.

"Okay," I said, pacing around the room now, but being careful not to get too close to the Destinos.

"Ah, *I've got it*," I continued. "Check her body. You shouldn't find a cut, a bruise, or any signs of struggle. I'm guessing he killed her with a kiss. That doesn't show up."

Luis shrugged.

"I wanna believe you, so I'll check it out."

"Please do," I said confidently.

I gladly stepped off to the side to let him by. I motioned for him to be my guest, which I then sort of regretted because it probably came off a little disrespectful.

He pulled her shirt back by the collar, and examined her shoulders, throat, and neck.

"What's this?" he asked, revealing a bruise she had, situated somewhere between her right shoulder and neck.

"*What?*" I asked, panicking. "*I have no...*"

He climbed off of the bed, swiveled his head in each direction to apparently crack his neck, and then reached for his gun.

"*Dude!*" I shouted, and then quickly looked to Angela for help. Her eyes were wide as well. I was used to her being a lot calmer; I needed her that way.

"*Wait!*" Kiki shouted. "The fight with the Rivers Street Girlz. That's probably where she got that bruise. *And* she got all spooked-out and claimed to see Angela herself that night at the crib, so it can't just be in his head. Feel me?"

He gave her a long, stern look.

"This is your girl lying here, you know," he said.

"*Whatcha sayin', Luis?*" she asked, suddenly irate.

Believe me, there is no mistaking whether or not a Latina is angry. I learned that over a relatively short period.

"You think I don't know that?" she continued, actually stepping to him.

Judging by his initial shock, I believe this was a first for the Destino-Destina family. Once he got his shit together, he puffed out his chest. I'd seen this type of behavior plenty of times before – on the Animal Network.

"Who you bringing the smoke to, girl?" he asked.

"She's just…" interrupted one of the Destinas.

Luis silenced her with his palm.

"Don't gas her up, Rosa," he said. "She doesn't need you co-signing for her."

Rosa nodded – silenced.

"Look," Kiki began once again, in a much calmer tone this time around. "All I'm saying is he's obviously been keeping it a hundred with us so far. And, I mean, we must be buying it on some level, right? Why else would we be here?"

"Yeah, but…" Luis motioned to Lil' Marie's body.

"I know," Kiki said.

"I wanna know as bad as you do, but I think something's going on that's much bigger than us. I mean, we're talkin' angels, Satan, and whoever else is involved. Whatever bodied Lil' Marie wasn't human, even though I guess he looked it, and I think it sure as hell wasn't Shawn.

"Don't you think if I actually thought it was him, I'd have pieced him myself by now? My nine is right in the next room."

She brought her gun into the house? This was news to me, but I guess I shouldn't have been *too* surprised. I mean, you can take the girl out of the hood... Plus, not that I thought it would be too much help, but I did figure it couldn't hurt to have it with us.

Nobody was clear with me regarding whether or not bullets could harm one of Satan's angels.

"*Okay*!" he blurted out. "What are we gonna do with her then?"

"Whatcha mean?" she asked, shrugging. "We can just call 9-1-1. This was 'natural causes,' right? We can't get in trouble for it."

His eyes widened.

"Yeah, it will definitely *look* like it was from natural causes," he agreed.

"But what isn't natural is she's the second Destina we've lost in the past week – not even. The boys are gonna know something's up. They'll be up our asses like crazy.

"No, girl, we can't take any chances. We'll take care of her."

Kiki hung her head low and rubbed her forehead. I could tell this was all getting to be a bit much for her. I mean, she *was* getting hit with a lot right off the bat.

In a weird way, I really felt like she and I had some sort of a connection now – and not the kind of connection that leads to flirting, if that's what you're thinking.

"Can the girls and I just have a minute with her first?" she asked, looking up into Luis's eyes.

"Of course, girl," he said. "Take all the time you need."

The Destinos filed out into the hallway. I followed, as did Angela. Luis didn't take his eyes off of me for the first minute or so. Fortunately, he no longer appeared angry with me.

"Crazy night, huh, bro?" he asked, forcing a smile.

I nodded. I didn't have much of anything to say to him yet. I had honestly thought he was going to kill me only a few minutes earlier.

"Hey, sorry about all that in there," he apologized. "Things just got a little crazy. I was having a tough time getting my shit together."

"It's okay," I finally said. I even grinned, oddly enough.

"What?" he asked, grinning himself a little.

"Nothing," I said. "I was just thinking at least you didn't kill me. That would've sucked."

He chuckled.

"Yeah," he agreed. "It definitely would have."

I wanted to ask him what they were going to do with Lil' Marie, but I knew better. Dealing with Luis was kind of like dealing with a pit bull. You just never knew what would set him off.

171

A few minutes later, the girls stepped out into the hallway. None of them had red eyes, which surprised me. I mean, wasn't she their girl? Sure, she was a pain in the butt with me, but surely they must've appreciated her on some level.

And it wasn't like the tears were there and they wiped them away; you can usually tell when that was the case.

"Okay, we're finished," Kiki informed Luis. "Be respectful, please."

"Of course," he said. "She's family."

"How are you gonna do it?" she asked. "Make it look like she OD'd on work?"

He shot me an uneasy glance, leading me to realize "work" was code for some sort of a drug – most likely something serious like crack.

I looked away from him in hopes of avoiding anything. Again, you never knew with a pit bull.

"Something like that," he said.

He then turned to me.

"I hate to do this to you, bro," he began, and I definitely grew worried. "But we really need the comforter from that bed. We figure we'll just wrap her up in it since she's already lying on it. Cool?"

"Yeah," I said, shrugging. "Whatever you need to do."

"Thanks," he said, gripping my shoulder kind of like a father might a son.

"*De nada,*" I replied, trying my best to let him know he didn't really need to worry about me.

If my nerves were even a little shot, I sincerely doubt I would've been able to go all bilingual on him like that.

He smiled, gave my right arm a pat, and maneuvered around me to enter the room. The others followed. A few of them shot me a look of gratitude – be it genuine or not.

I was kind of torn now. By allowing all of this to go on, was I doing something wrong?

I feel a little naïve saying this – and I swear it isn't some sort of a cop-out – but the line was definitely blurred here. I mean, they didn't actually kill her, but it still felt as though they were covering something up.

Was I being intimidated into thinking they weren't *really* doing anything wrong, or was I just trying to go easy on myself? She was a casualty in the war against Satan, and this was just another way of burying their dead – albeit a shady way.

I found something to do while they were carrying her out. I emptied the dishwasher, which needed to be done anyways – whatever I needed to tell myself, I guess.

The next few days were mostly made up of downtime.

They consisted of a lot of Bible reading for Michelle and me and a lot of catching up on television shows for Kiki. She was always leaving that damn television on; more often than not, she'd leave the room with it still on and not make her way back in there for hours.

Once Saturday rolled around, I was looking for any reason to get out of that house, which I'm sure sounds odd considering I was sharing it with three attractive young women – one of whom was a legit angel.

Believe me, though, it looked much better on paper.

They complained about the state of the bathroom (which until then had always been a bachelor's bathroom), they complained about the lack of meals I prepared (even though I bought all of the food *and* cleared the table and counters), and finally, they did most of this complaining in Spanish initially; I needed to wait for them to calm down some before I heard in English what I had done wrong.

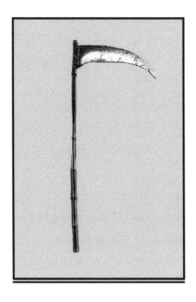

Chapter 13
Angela

Marie's Place was just how I remembered it. It smelled like a bunch of different kinds of food thrown together – none of them prepared particularly well.

There were a few complaints here and there, but for the most part, the diners had the expected "beggars can't be choosers" mentality. They appreciated this break.

Michelle really looked pleased with herself; good for her. She wasn't too chatty with the people she served, but she was loaded with smiles for them.

In fact, she received a lot of compliments on her smile, which I'm sure made her feel good considering the shape her face was still in. It was the other set of compliments she received that *really* blew her mind.

"You're such a thoughtful young lady," said one woman.

"It's *so* refreshing to see young kids like you helping out around here," said another.

And, finally, "I tell ya, I wish *my* daughter was more like you."

This last one nearly caused her to drop the stack of trays she was carrying. I can only imagine what something like this does for a former gangsta.

She was beaming as she hurried into the kitchen. I'm not sure what the rush was. From where I stood, I couldn't really tell whether or not her face was red. She may have just not wanted anything to spoil the moment. I was so happy for her.

Shawn, on the other hand, spent as much time as he could out there; the dining area was definitely his stage. The ladies adored him, especially the older ones. Why, a few of them even showed him pictures of their daughters and granddaughters. And I'm not gonna lie. I looked at most of them over his shoulder.

He glanced back at me a few times and winked; I don't think anyone caught it, though. They would have said something. I know I had no reason to be jealous, but still, I was.

I already knew he was a sweet guy, but he had definitely upped his game, there was no denying it. I mean, let's be honest. When more than one complete stranger's trying to hook you up with her granddaughter, you're obviously a catch.

I know Michael warned me about this, but I had a difficult time just ignoring my feelings on it. What do you want? Shawn was a great guy.

And, you have to remember that my father split before I had the chance to get to know him, so it took me a long time to give *any* guy the chance to be great.

Of course, Mama didn't help by never dating again, but honestly, who could blame her? He must've done a number on her, the son of a bitch. Sorry, Lord, but I just get so…

Now and then, whenever I really start getting pissed off at my old man, who may or may not have been one of my mourners (Michael never told me), I need to calm myself down and the best sedative for that just happens to be Shawn memories now, my favorite of which is probably that of him slow-dancing with one of the old ladies who didn't have a picture to show him that day.

She was feeling a little left out, or so he thought, so he invited her out to the open area near the entrance to the room for a little dance.

"I'm not any good, mind you," he said. "But…"

"I'll show you how," she said, smiling away.

Do you wanna hear something crazy? Not one of the Destinas showed any interest in him.

Maybe it was because they were all spoken for or because they knew he was dying, but either way, I was still a little surprised.

They were more into those jerks who treated them like *caca* than they were this poor guy who had opened his freaking house to them. I mean, how do you do that?

I'm glad Luis never ended up sending one of them up to his room because I honestly don't know whether or not he would've sent her away.

I mean, when your days are numbered like that, I'll bet there are things you might consider that you typically wouldn't – such as having sex with somebody you don't necessarily share an emotional bond with.

Anyways, rant over; back to the task at hand – volunteering at Marie's Place. Things were going great there up until Michelle noticed a familiar face all strung-out on something stumble through the double-doors.

"Shawn!" she shouted, hurrying over to where we stood. "Hey, Shawn!"

177

"What's up?" he asked, smiling to beat the band. OMG, I was even using his expressions now.

He wasn't really flirting with her or anything like that. He was just smiling at her because he was so happy for her.

An hour or so earlier, he drew attention to how happy and even "fulfilled" she seemed.

This was a good look for somebody like her. Fulfilled.

"Kiki's mom just walked in," she explained in a hurry. "Well, she barely walked in, I should say."

"*Really?*" he asked, incredulously.

He began scanning the area closest to the door. At first glance, he came up empty-handed, but she stood out after a while.

It was just like when you have to stare at one of those pictures for a while before what you're looking for appears.

"Is that her trying to squeeze in on the end there?" he asked, hoping it wasn't.

"Yup," Michelle confirmed. "She wasn't always like this, just so you know."

"Let us not therefore judge one another anymore," he muttered.

Kiki's mom looked like she was struggling to keep just one cheek on the end of the bench. The woman next to her wouldn't budge. In all fairness, it didn't look like she had much extra room to give.

"This is great!" he exclaimed, with unbridled excitement in his eyes even though he didn't expect to have there.

"We can bring her back with us."

"Are you crazy?" Michelle asked, as though she too now owned the place. Even I didn't make myself *that* comfortable. "And deal with Kiki?"

"What?" he asked. "She's been…"

Michelle interrupted him with a head shake.

"I say we go home at the end of our shift or whenever, figure out what we're gonna say to her, and then just tell her," she suggested. "Okay?"

"She's right," I agreed.

"Okay," was all he said.

The poor thing thought he was really on to something there. I really felt for him. His heart was in it, that's for sure.

While they were helping to clean up, Michael showed up and pulled me aside.

"Our boy's doing well, isn't he?" he said.

"*I* think so," I answered.

I kind of liked hearing him referred to as "our boy." I felt like I had a deeper, more personal connection with him as the result.

Michael sighed.

"There's really nothing I can say to dissuade you from falling for him, is there?" he asked.

"I tried," I replied. "I wish I literally *couldn't* fall for him. It doesn't seem fair… to either of us."

"I won't comment on that, other than to say that this is God's rule for a reason," he explained. "You need to understand that."

"So then, it *is* set in stone?" I asked.

He grinned, and then quoted Matthew for me.

"For when the dead rise, they will neither marry nor be given in marriage. In this respect they will be like angels in Heaven."

Marriage? I never said anything about being his wife. *Sweet.* I thought I may have found a loophole there.

"You know He doesn't deal in semantics, young lady," Michael interrupted. "Nor does he leave room for 'loopholes.' As I've said before, you can *develop* these feelings; you just can't *act* upon them. I was hoping this understanding alone would be enough for you to restrain yourself."

I had a difficult time focusing on what he said right after that because Shawn coincidentally picked that moment to begin horsing around with me.

What he did was he tapped me on my right shoulder and snuck off. As a human, I might have fallen for it; as an angel, the list of culprits was limited. He was such a goof ball.

"Yup," Michael said. "You're hopeless."

I batted my eyelashes. He wasn't amused.

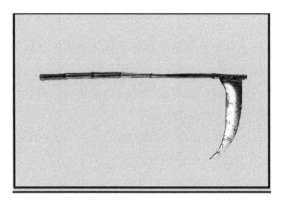

Chapter 14
Shawn

I don't know why the heck I did that to myself; the flirting with Angela, I mean. Even if she did get "earthly desires" anymore, it's not like we could have done anything about them.

Still, I'm not going to lie, I definitely wished she could still get them because I thought we had pretty good chemistry going. This hadn't happened with too many other girls I'd been acquainted with – maybe two or three tops, so I knew it when I felt it, but even with them, I can't say it clicked like this.

I definitely liked this girl – sorry, *woman*. It's funny, she was around eighteen and I still referred to her as a "girl." However, when I was that age only a year or so earlier, *I* was unmistakably a man.

The way she looked at me from time to time, I'm pretty sure she knew I had feelings for her.

She never actually addressed them, but you can tell when a girl knows you like her.

She either flashes you the *I won* grin the first few times she sees you after realizing it, or she tries to avoid being alone with you – which would obviously be no easy task for her since I was the only one who could see and speak with her anymore.

"You need to try to shake those feelings," she finally explained to me once we got back from volunteering.

I nodded. Denied, yet again. However, I treated it like it was just a reminder from the first time. This softened the blow a little.

I couldn't shake those feelings, though. I mean, come on. She was gorgeous. She had those nice, almond-shaped, light brown eyes that weren't *too too* big. She had that petite sort of body, but it wasn't too young-looking (in other words, I wouldn't have felt creepy about it).

And finally, she had her hair pulled back into a ponytail like every time I saw her, which might not have been by choice. Regardless, it was a look I loved.

To be honest with you, I couldn't even picture her with all of that crazy make-up the other two had on that time. You know, the time I'm not particularly fond of?

"I'm all of a sudden struggling with that," I admitted. "Which I know is stupid because it's not like you can even get these feelings for somebody – no matter who he is."

She was unresponsive. I wasn't quite sure what to make of this, but I didn't force the issue. I mean, what would have been the point?

"When are you gonna talk to Kiki?" she asked quickly, probably trying to escape the awkwardness.

I stared at her for a moment like I had just missed an opportunity, which was pretty much a waste of time considering the opportunity in question was kind of null and void to begin with.

I felt like she had me in a precarious position, even though I guess she really didn't. I mean, it wasn't exactly up to her. I was all jammed up, no two ways about it.

She tilted her head to the side, pouting away like a little girl.

"I just feel so bad," she said.

"Don't," I said. "It is what it is."

I sighed.

Back to the business at hand. "I'll talk it over with Michelle to see how she thinks we should bring it up to her."

"Okay," she said. "If you want my input, though, I think you should just flat out tell her. You don't wanna beat around the bush on something like this. She'd probably be pissed if you did."

"Hmm, you might be right," I agreed. "Something like that might get me *pieced*."

"Not bad, white boy," Angela said, with a cute little smirk. Oh, boy; it used to just be a smirk; now, it was a *cute little* smirk. I warned myself to snap out of it.

"You will," she sighed. "Give it time."

She didn't look very pleased over the probability of me losing those feelings. What did it matter to her, though, if she couldn't reciprocate them?

I figured it was strictly on my behalf she was disappointed; perhaps she felt bad for me.

Within ten minutes, Michelle and I were seated across from Kiki at the dining room table. From the time I invited her to join us there to the time I finally hit her with the reason behind this little sit-down of ours, she looked a little suspicious.

"Okay," I began. "Here's what's going on. Today, at Marie's Place, we saw your mother."

After all that had gone on recently, we discovered it was still possible to shock her. Her eyes widened. She looked a little pissed, too.

183

"*My* mother was there?" she asked, practically fuming now. "Was she there alone?"

Michelle fielded this one.

"I'm pretty sure," she said. "I didn't see any dudes with her, if that's what you mean."

Kiki nodded, looking a *little* closer to satisfied. I'm thinking she either had a pimp or a pusher in mind.

Kiki quickly glanced up at the clock on the wall.

"Do you think she's still there?" she asked.

"I doubt it," I said, looking up there myself. It had been a little over an hour and a half probably since I saw her mother take a seat at the end of that bench. I figured it was one of those chew and screw type scenarios.

"Who knows, though?" I continued. "She might be back for dinner. I mean, they probably serve breakfast, lunch, and dinner there. Wouldn't you think?"

"Yeah," she said, growing a little excited. "You're probably right. We should head over there in like an hour."

I nodded. It sounded like the right move to me.

She turned to me for a moment. "No offense, but can you give Michelle and me a little privacy? There's something I wanna ask her about."

"Yeah," I said. "No problem."

I left the table and made my way right upstairs. This way, I couldn't be tempted to eavesdrop, which has always been a bad habit of mine.

And I'm not sure I wanted to find out what happens to you when you're caught eavesdropping on gangstas – well, one gangsta anyways.

I figured what better time to bring Angela up to speed.

From out in the hallway, I heard a muffled cry coming from her bedroom. Actually, I'm not sure "muffled" was the best way to describe it.

184

I'd say a better description would be she was *struggling* to cry; she obviously wanted to, but she just couldn't get it out.

I used to get this way whenever I faked a crying fit in hopes of gathering sympathy from my parents. It never worked for me.

This was different, though. It wasn't malicious; how could it be, really?

I needed more, so I stepped to the door and just about pressed my ear to it – what did I tell you about my eavesdropping? She was clearly distraught over something. It was very unlike her. Well, it was unlike the her I was accustomed to anyways.

"*It's not fair*," she said. "Why even let me have emotions anymore if I can't do anything about them?"

Silence.

"I know He trusts me, and I'm glad He does, but still…"

Silence.

"No, he doesn't know," she continued. She must have been talking about me, I figured. "I'm just glad he hasn't straight-up asked me, because it's not like I can lie anymore."

Once it dawned on me that the repercussions could be potentially worse should two Angels of Death catch me eavesdropping, I did an about face and snuck back downstairs.

They probably knew I was there, though. Well, Michael probably knew, anyways.

I felt like a man without a home, literally. I couldn't go to the dining room – or even the kitchen since it was within earshot of them – and I couldn't stay upstairs.

The living room it was – or the "library" if you ever asked my grandfather; he figured fifteen or so books on a shelf earned a room the title of library.

Only one of the books in there really mattered to me anymore, so I picked a random page – Mark 3. It was chock-filled with Jesus' parables. There were some tricky ones in there; at least, they were tricky for me.

185

I read them a few times over and sort of got lost in them.

Sometime later, I noticed the shadow of a hand race across the page. I looked up to find Kiki waving her hand up and down before me.

"Yo, white boy," she said, with a smile. "You still with us?"

I snapped out of it, nodding in pretty much the same motion she waved.

She chuckled.

"Cute," she said.

I'm not going to lie; I did blush a little. Michelle simply rolled her eyes.

"We're ready whenever you are," she continued.

I shot right up on my feet, ever the obedient puppy. Pathetic. Kiki patted me atop the head.

"Good boy," she joked. "And I didn't even need to jiggle your car keys."

"Lol. Very funny," I said. "Let's go."

On our way there, she hit me with an unexpected question.

"Um, why are you so eager to help *my* mother? Michelle said that earlier today you were so amped up to help that you wanted to bring her back to the house right away.

"How come? You don't even know her or what kind of problems she might have brought in with her. I mean, let's be honest; you barely know *us*."

Suddenly, Mark 3:33 jumped into my head.

"One day, Jesus was preaching to a bunch of people, in a synagogue, I think," I began.

"Anyways, somebody told Him His mother and brothers were outside, and they wanted to see Him. Well, Jesus looks at the guy and asks him, 'Who is my mother and who are my brothers?'

"Then, He looks around at all the people in there and answers His own question. He says, 'Here are my mother and my brothers. Anyone who obeys God is my brother or sister or mother.'

"So, there you have it. That's why."

She nodded. Whether or not she understood, who knows? I'm thinking she did.

"Well, even though I think you're not all there, good looks," she said.

I chuckled, and took the right down the street Marie's Place was on.

Kiki hesitated a moment before exiting the car. To be honest with you, she looked as though she'd lost a lot of her drive. I felt bad because she *was* so dead set on confronting her mom.

"Well?" I asked, for some stupid reason.

Sometimes, I wish I thought these things through before I said them.

"*Gimme a minute,*" she said, a little peeved. "I'm debating whether or not to bring the smoke to her."

When we finally made our way in there, only a few of that evening's diners had arrived. I guess we were a little early.

Not long after the place started filling up, Kiki's mom scrambled through the double doors, looking in just as rough a shape as she had earlier.

Her hair looked a little more unkempt; this was the only difference I noticed.

"Oh, Mama," Kiki said, shaking her head in disbelief.

We all watched as the poor woman searched a seat out. The looks on some of the other diners' faces as she shuffled by led me to believe she was mighty ripe. Kiki had a similar expression.

"Well, no sense in dragging this out," she said, and then started toward her mom, who still hadn't found a seat.

I hung back, as did Michelle; this obviously wasn't our fight. I could tell Kiki started in on her mother as soon as she reached her. Not that I'm any kind of an expert lip reader anyways, but she had her back to us, so I had no idea what she was saying to her.

She was animated, that's for sure. There was a lot of talking with her hands, to the point where her mom definitely appeared overwhelmed, and even a bit confused.

"Her mom doesn't recognize her," Michelle said. She had a better read on her.

Kiki's body language did suggest that she was trying to jog her mom's memory. She continuously patted her own chest with her right hand while gripping her mom's shoulder with her left.

Her mom repeatedly tried to jerk herself free. The dazed look in her eyes was evidence enough for me that this was no performance; this poor woman honestly did not recognize her daughter.

Poor Kiki.

Eventually, she, now clearly agitated, forced a couple of women to move down on the bench for her mom. These women, I assure you, wanted no part of Kiki, especially not right then.

She stormed out of the room once her mom took her seat. We soon joined her outside. She was waiting for us at the car.

Kiki didn't utter a word the entire way home. She didn't have to; Michelle and I had pretty much figured it all out.

Either her mom couldn't handle the stress of being a single mother any longer, so she pretended the drugs had stripped her entirely of her memories, or she really was so far gone that she could no longer recognize her own daughter.

Neither possibility was any better than the other, in my opinion.

She waited until we were alone to finally break her silence.

"I need you," she said.

This was unexpected. I'm guessing my face gave me away, again.

"*Not like that*," she corrected. "Sorry. What I mean is I need you to talk to Angela for me, sort of like a medium or whatever they're called. Can you do that? It's really important."

She looked very determined. Whatever she had in mind must have come to her on the ride home.

"Yeah," I agreed. "I can do that. Sure."

"Yeah, that's fine," Angela added, sort of sneaking up behind me.

"*Oh*," I said, a little wide-eyed. "Speak of the… er… angel."

I turned to take a gander at her, and then backed up so they were standing face to face. Well, in a matter of speaking. At least from my perspective they were.

"Um, how do we do this?" Kiki asked, looking about as vulnerable as I'd ever seen her.

"Well," I began. "I guess you can just ask her whatever you want to ask her, and I'll let you know what her response is."

Both girls appeared satisfied with this approach.

"Okay," Kiki said. "I'll just put it out there. Angela, can you please kill my mom?"

Angela backed up a step, as did I. Kiki acknowledged my reaction and immediately attempted to rectify her request.

"Can you *save* her? That's what I mean. I think she's headed down the wrong path, and I don't want her to end up in Hell.

"She's a good woman, she really is. She's just screwed-up in the head now because of the drugs. I'm just worried she's gonna start doing stuff she shouldn't be doing to support her drug habit, if she ain't already."

She waited a moment to allow Angela a chance to respond. Angela, of course, was speechless. I mean, neither one of us were expecting something like this.

"Well?" Kiki asked. "Is she saying anything yet?"

I shook her off and waited patiently.

"Don't you think we should maybe try to get her some help first?" Angela asked. "I mean, this seems a little extreme."

189

I repeated this for Kiki. I wasn't even finished before she was shaking her head.

"She'll never go for that," she complained. "She doesn't even recognize me. Remember?"

She was pretty desperate now – even more so than before.

"And I just don't think she has a lot of time," she added. "She looked pretty rough. You saw."

I did, and I'm afraid she was right.

"I don't know about this, Shawn," Angela said. "I just don't. Tell her I need a few minutes to think it over, okay?"

I nodded. Angela walked off and climbed the stairs. She seemed really nerve-racked over this, which didn't look promising for Kiki.

I had to deliver the news. "She isn't sure about this. She just went upstairs to mull it over."

Kiki nodded dejectedly. This obviously wasn't the answer she wanted to hear, but it could have been much worse. She could have gotten the "no" right away.

After a few awkward minutes of waiting – during which time I looked just about everywhere in the room except into Kiki's eyes, I decided to check on Angela.

"I'll go see what the holdup is," I said.

"Okay," she began. "Just don't be too pushy up there, okay?"

"I won't," I said. "Don't worry."

She nodded, and I headed on up.

Angela was pacing around her room when I got up there. I could tell she was stressing like crazy over this.

"I don't think I can do this," she said. "Can I?"

"You're asking *me*?" I said, dumbfounded.

Even this she looked unsure of.

"No, I guess not," she began. "I was just looking for a second opinion. That's all."

"Well, my honest opinion is that you should go for it," I said, hoping I hadn't upset anyone – namely Michael or the Lord.

"How come?" she asked.

"There was a woman at my grandfather's nursing home who had Alzheimer's," I began.

"It's a nursing home, Shawn," she said. "I'm sure there are plenty of people there with Alzheimer's. It happens."

"Um, can I finish?" I said, trying not to sound too rude about it.

She nodded.

"The difference is I think this woman was still in her fifties when she got it," I continued. "That's pretty young to be getting Alzheimer's, don't you think?"

Again, she nodded, and allowed me to continue.

"Anyways, her daughter, who I figured was only a little older than us, popped in for a visit pretty much every time I was there and probably even more often than that. Meanwhile, this poor woman had no idea who she was.

"Her daughter had gotten to be completely unrecognizable to her. Their interactions broke my heart. I mean, imagine what it would be like if you were still alive and all of a sudden your mother forgot who you were, and you were forced to watch her die a slow death that could potentially go on for years.

"You would hate it, right?"

"Yes," she answered.

"At least this woman could visit with her mother every day if she wanted to, and she could take comfort in the fact that she was surrounded by people who were taking care of her, or at the very least trying to.

"Kiki, meanwhile, goes days, maybe even weeks, without seeing her mother. And, I'll bet more often than not her mom's at some crack house surrounded by dealers, who don't give a rat's ass about her well-being, and other junkies, who probably can't wait for her to die, so they can rob her, providing she even has anything worth taking anymore."

"I'll do it," Angela said, with a sigh.

I didn't even respond. Instead, I motioned for her to follow me downstairs.

Kiki needed to hear this ASAP.

"She'll do it," I announced, incredulously. "Wow!"

Kiki's eyes lit up. She *clearly* wasn't expecting this, nor was I obviously.

"You seem as surprised as me," I said, staring at a now relieved Kiki.

"I just didn't think she would," she admitted.

"I didn't know if this was like breaking one of God's rules or something."

"Yeah, well, just tell her about Jesus healing the guy with the crippled hand on the Sabbath," Angela said. "This is why I decided to do it."

I nodded and turned to Kiki.

"One day, on the Sabbath – a day nobody was supposed to work, a guy with a crippled hand walked up to Jesus and asked Him to heal his hand. Meanwhile, the Pharisees 'the head Jews' were waiting for Jesus to do something He wasn't supposed to; they figured this would be it.

"Anyways, Jesus goes ahead and heals the guy, and they're loving every minute of it. They call Him on it pretty much right away. Then, He says this to them: 'On the Sabbath should we do good deeds, or evil deeds? Should we save someone's life or destroy it?'

"She'd rather save your mom's life than let her destroy it. Feel me?"

She nodded.

Needless to say, I loved relaying this particular message.

"We'll see if she shows up at Marie's Place tomorrow, and, if she does, I'll take it from there," Angela explained.

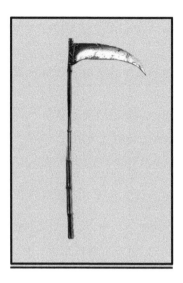

Chapter 15
Angela

I was pretty nervous from the instant I agreed to this. Was I completely breaking from protocol, or was there even a protocol to break from?

We were pulling into the Marie's Place parking lot the next morning during their breakfast hours and Michael still hadn't intervened, leading me to believe he was fine with it.

He could have at least made an appearance, I thought. I mean, I realize this was basically a mercy killing, but it wasn't exactly a sanctioned one. I would have felt a lot more at ease if he had just given me his blessing and taken off.

On the drive there, Kiki was more on edge than she was the night they did the drive-by. Granted, this *was* her flesh and blood she'd essentially put a hit on. She was fidgety. It's a good thing she wasn't packing.

"Hey, um, tell Angela I really appreciate this, okay?" she barely managed to say.

"And, well, you know, good looks."

"You just did," Shawn said, smiling.

"Also, um, you can tell her I wanna show her how much this means to me."

"How?" he asked.

"I'm gonna try to boost my image, like we talked about," she said.

"You know, by doing more good stuff like working here and whatnot."

He nodded.

"Good idea."

"Yeah," she agreed. "I just feel like I gotta do something to change. Feel me? This isn't…"

She stared them down. Michelle and Shawn, I mean.

"What?" he asked.

She shook her head, dismissing whatever she had in mind.

"*Hey*, you can tell us," he added.

She took a deep breath and gave Michelle one last look before sharing.

"Okay, here goes. This isn't really working out for me anymore. This life, I mean. Hmm, never thought I'd say that. I *was* for it. Now, I don't know anymore. It's just…"

Again, she shook her head.

It didn't even matter to me that she couldn't finish this thought. I think I knew where she was headed, and I was feeling much better about doing this favor for her.

And I'm guessing Michael knew this decision loomed in her mind. Maybe *this* was why he didn't call me on it.

There weren't many diners for breakfast. The one who mattered most was there, though.

Shawn pointed her out to me. I'd seen her before, but she looked a lot different now. The girls hung back in the car, waiting for his return. He jokingly cracked the windows for them.

They weren't amused. He just wanted to lighten the mood some.

As expected, though, Kiki wasn't really in the mood to have hers lightened. Michelle got that. Shawn didn't. He never does. Let's just say tact isn't exactly his thing.

"So?" he began. "What's the plan?"

"The plan is you're going back to the car, letting Kiki know what's up, and then the three of you are going back to the house to chill," I explained.

"I have no idea how long this will take. I mean, I can't just do it *here*. I don't want to run the risk of them having to shut this place down – even if it's just for a little while for an investigation."

He knew I raised a good point. And he's so cute. He gave me a quick hug. He didn't care what it may have looked like to onlookers, which was nice.

He even closed his eyes, so he wouldn't have to deal with them.

"Be careful," he whispered, just before he released me.

Whatever they served up that morning was sort of a mystery to me. I didn't think soup kitchens really got cute like that, I figured they'd want to make it as boring and economical as possible.

It's a shame Kiki's mom probably had no idea what she was eating for a last meal. There was egg involved somehow, that much I could tell.

Whatever it was, she took one reluctant bite, stood up and walked to the trash with it.

She gave one last look at the place as though she knew – even though she couldn't have. I took this as a signal I should head for the doors.

Once outside, she took a seat on the curb and brought her knees together like she was cold. I sat down next to her and waited; for what, I didn't know. I just didn't want to take her yet, neither there nor then.

I kind of needed her away from Marie's Place. The further, the better.

After a minute or so of staring at the cars in an adjoining parking lot – some nice, some just so-so, she surprised me by pulling a phone out of her pocket and dialing somebody up.

I leaned over to check the screen, but nobody's name appeared, just the numbers she punched in. How'd *she* get a phone? And more importantly, who was she calling?

"Hey, it's me," she said, gloomily. "I'm ready whenever."

She ended the call and waited, scratching her arm a few times in the process – further evidence, I thought.

I had a decision to make now: when to take her. I mean, did I really want to see who was picking us up and where we were headed?

Part of me didn't want to, but the rest of me needed to feel better about what I was doing. Again, a visit from Michael would have been very helpful at this point.

Twenty or so minutes later, a black Mustang pulled up. There was a light-skinned brotha a little on the skinny side behind the wheel. He was alone. She opened the passenger side door and we both slid in.

It reeked of weed inside; he must have smoked up on his way there. She checked out his ashtray. Looking for a roach, I assume.

"You couldn't have saved me any?" she asked, clearly agitated.

"That's real."

"Whatchu care, bitch?" he sneered. "Dope is a gateway drug. You already through the gates."

He chuckled.

"Shoot, you can't even *see* the damn gates anymore you so far past 'em."

All she could do was shake her head and then scratch it some.

"Well, then," she began, a little testy now. "Give me something that *is* more my speed."

He chuckled, once again, which was as annoying as it was cruel.

"Not so fast," he said. "You know how we do. 'Round here, you gotta earn if you wanna burn. Ain't nothin' changed about that. I don't care if you did lose your house. No freebies. The trap house can wait; we gonna hit up my boy's crib first. He got someone there that wants to get to *know* you."

She hung her head in shame.

"Not now," she muttered. It was barely audible. "I'm too tired for that shit."

He simply grinned, the bastard. I guess this was better than how I thought he'd react, though.

Then again, whoever was waiting for her probably wanted her face intact; no bloody lip or anything like that.

"He's a good twenty minutes away," he said. "So, why don't you just adjust your seat a little and take a little nap? I'll wake you when we get there."

She went ahead and did just that. She closed her eyes, and I took this opportunity to make sure she wouldn't open them again. I leaned over and planted one right on her cheek.

"Please welcome her into Your Kingdom of Heaven, Father," I whispered.

We weren't too far from where Mama lived, maybe a few miles tops, when he realized something was wrong. When he pulled over and hurried around to check on her, I left. I took solace in the fact that I'd spared her one last mistake with a pervert.

It was on to Mama's now. I hadn't seen her since my funeral.

I felt bad I hadn't checked in on her. I mean, I really had no idea how she was handling all of this; it hadn't been long.

"It's not your fault," Michael said, suddenly strolling alongside me. "You've been pretty busy lately."

"Thanks," I said. "It's no excuse, though. My sleepless nights would have been better spent watching over her."

"She's been fine," he explained. "Nothing to concern yourself with. You'll see."

I figured it wouldn't be too out of line if I asked his opinion of what I'd done for Kiki.

"I'm guessing you saw what I just did," I said.

"Of course," he said. He didn't appear disappointed in me.

"You did a noble thing for your friend," he said. "We'll leave it at that."

"So, you're not mad at me?" I asked, unable to leave it alone.

He rolled his eyes, which I guess I deserved. I suppose I *was* being a pest who couldn't – or wouldn't – take a hint.

"You did the right thing, Angela," he said.

"Everyone agrees. Otherwise, you wouldn't have been able to do it. He put you in that position and He knew just how you would handle it."

I sighed, relieved. This whole time I was afraid I'd be fired or written up or whatever.

Michael smirked.

"No, dear," he said. "It takes a lot more than this to lose your role. I mean, don't go on any mercy killing sprees or anything like that, but…"

"I understand," I said, interrupting him.

Shoot! Perhaps it wasn't my best decision to interrupt an angel, especially when he's my boss.

"I'm not your boss," he said, clearly amused over how prone to worrying I was.

"We have the same boss, and He's approved of your performance thus far. He likes that you went with your heart on this one. It's going to prove more beneficial than you think."

I was pleased, yet sort of confused.

"Meaning?" I asked.

"You'll see," he said. "For now, just enjoy some alone time with your mother."

He motioned to our front door. I'd been so engulfed in our conversation I didn't even notice we'd arrived.

I turned to thank him, but he was already gone. I couldn't wait to master that; I could have some fun with Shawn with it. Then again, *he'd* probably get a kick out of it. He *was* one of those phantom shoulder-tappers, if you recall, and something like this had the potential to take that trick to the next level.

Of course, Michael probably wouldn't be too pleased with me.

Suddenly, I felt a tap upon my shoulder. I turned to face the music, but he wasn't there to reprimand me. I chuckled. What do you know? I guess he did have a sense of humor after all.

Go figure.

Mama was in her easy chair, reading a newspaper of all things. I only say this because I can't remember ever having seen one in our home; the closest we'd come were the weekly grocery store fliers.

Nope. This was definitely new territory.

She was up to the obituaries when I got there, or perhaps she started with them. I have no idea.

"*Twenty-five*?" she said. "*Ay Dios Mio*. Too young."

Too young? Yeah, I guess so. He made it further than I did, though, whoever he was.

"Eighty-three," she continued, clearly satisfied. "That's more like it."

I shook my head in slight disbelief. I guess this was how she mourned. I was sort of hoping this wasn't some sort of a routine for her, but the stack of newspapers resting on the coffee table confirmed my fear.

Why was she putting herself through this? This couldn't have been all that therapeutic.

It sucked that there was nothing I could do for her. Really, the only thing I could think of was to stand behind her with my hands on her shoulders.

Hopefully, this would prove to be a calming presence for her in some fashion. I wasn't quite sure how it worked. She turned her head slightly, so maybe this was a sign it was working.

I convinced myself it was.

It would've probably been easier to just visit her in a dream, but I didn't know if this was even still an option and I really needed to be back at the house since Kiki was probably waiting with bated breath for word of her mom's passing.

It wouldn't have been right to keep her waiting too long.

I was just hoping she wouldn't ask me for any of the details. There were certain truths I felt people could live without. This, of course, isn't how I feel anymore.

I bent over Mama and was just about to kiss her goodbye atop the head, which had always been a habit of mine, when it suddenly dawned on me that this was no longer an option – not unless I wanted to end her life.

Man, did this suck sometimes.

They were *all* seated in the living room. I mean every one of the Destinas – all five of them. It's hard to believe the number had dropped by two so quickly.

I mean, sure, some of the elder Destinas were still around, but they weren't up to much these days. They were mostly Destina in name only, from what I gathered. It seemed like being *for that* catches up with you after a while.

Like anything else, I think it's probably a young person's game.

Shawn stood up right away when I stepped into the room as though I were royalty. I motioned for him to sit back down, and he did.

"She's here," he blurted out. I think they were already hip, though, thanks to his initial reaction.

"Did you… you know?" he asked.

I nodded solemnly. Not that I wasn't satisfied, but it's nothing to be pleased about. It is what it is.

"She did," he passed on to Kiki and the others.

She let out a sigh of relief. A tear trickled down her cheek.

"Can I tell her what we discussed?" he asked. Man, was he gassed.

"Calm down," Kiki replied, wiping her tears away. "Yes, you can tell her."

She reached for Rosa's hand, confusing me. It didn't seem like it was just for emotional support; it had a different feel to it.

Shawn quickly turned to me, his eyes lit.

"They're finished," he said.

They all looked to each other for what seemed like one last time.

"Finished with what?" I asked.

"Oh, sorry," he apologized, with what seemed like an almost nervous sort of energy.

"Kiki decided to leave the gang because of what you did for her. I didn't even need to ask her. Can you believe it?"

No. This was unbelievable. No wonder he was so eager to share. It's not that this was so unfathomable; I just didn't think it would be this easy.

Actually, I shouldn't put it that way. I mean, rescuing Kiki's mom's soul *was* a big deal, I just figured I'd need to do more, like take on a Satanic angel or two.

"And all of the others are on board, too?" I asked, glancing around the room.

"Yeah," he said. "They weren't too sure about it at first, but none of them really want this anymore. In fact, Kiki was the reason most of them were still sticking it out. They didn't want to let her down, especially since she's had to deal with a lot on their behalf recently.

"When she said she was leaving the Destinas, they were actually pretty relieved. I still can't get over it. I told her she should have retired or whatever a while ago."

"The only reason I'm doing this is because of what she did for me," Kiki admitted.

"I figure it's the least I can do. I'm ready to follow you guys or Jesus or whoever. Just make it worth it, okay? Please. For all of us. We've really put ourselves out there. Feel me?"

"It'll totally be worth it," he said, much calmer now. "Trust me."

She sighed, once again.

"I guess the only thing left to do now is convince Luis to let us go," she said.

Oh, no. I wondered what *that* entailed.

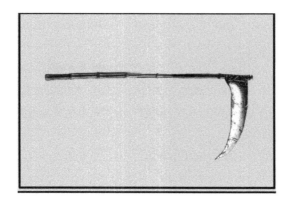

<u>Chapter 16</u>
Shawn

We needed to convince Luis to *let* them go?

"Look," I began, pretty agitated now. I'd gone from being in a great mood to this.

"You're not slaves. He doesn't own you."

Kiki only balked at this notion.

"No!" I exclaimed. "Don't do that. I've had enough of people doing that."

By people, I think I meant anybody who had ever balked at me for as far back as I could remember. People like my uncle, my aunt, the hospice nurse, Kiki, and even Angela. I'd had enough.

"I'm sorry," she apologized. "You just don't get it, though. This is how it is. It's how it's always been."

"Well, then, what do we have to do?" I asked. I couldn't let this slip through my fingers. Mentally, we had them, but we obviously needed them physically as well; mind, body, and soul.

"I don't know," she said, a little sad-eyed. "I've never even considered this before. I always figured I'd die a Destina, either too young or too old."

"Too old?" I asked. "Isn't it the goal to die old?"

I could tell she was about to balk, again, but she must have caught herself. This train of thought was probably too ass-backward to assume most people felt the same.

"This probably isn't the case with most gangs – or maybe it is, I don't know, but Destina elders really don't get the respect they deserve," she admitted.

"They never have from what we've been told, and unfortunately, they're fine with it. At least, they act like it's all good. It's really chips, though, if you ask me. I mean, how could it not be? I don't want it for myself or any of my girls.

"They look pathetic, walking around with their sad, old faces all done up Chola-style. It looks good on a younger face, but it looks scary on an older face – and not the good kind of scary. Feel me?

"It ain't no life for me. And the Destinos don't even stick with them after a while. They wait around for the younger ones to come up. You see, seniority actually means something to them; they get their pick of the litter.

"That's nothing to look forward to.

"For the longest time, I thought there were only a few ways to break away from that litter and none of them looked too appealing. There was either death, gettin' jumped out like Michelle, or well, the way my Mom did it.

"Thank God you and Angela came into the picture, that's all I have to say. I mean, you changed everything for me – for us. We just need to figure out how to do this now."

"That's the million-dollar question, isn't it?" I asked, a little concerned, but still about as determined as I'd ever been.

"I think you need to have a little sit-down with Luis," Angela suggested.

204

She was right. I kind of figured this was the case. I just didn't know what I was going to say to him just yet.

I mean, he was somewhat nice to me so far in our relationship because he probably didn't consider me a viable threat. That all changed, though, once the girls agreed to give up their Destina lifestyle for a relationship with the Lord.

Kiki noticed how distressed I was; I didn't hide it well. A worrywart never does.

"What's wrong, Shawn?" she asked. "You look a little unsure of something."

Now *she* looked a little concerned. No doubt she wondered if *I* was all of a sudden having second thoughts.

"I'm not unsure of what we're doing, if that's what you're thinking," I quickly reassured her. "I'm just trying to figure out the best approach. I'm thinking I need to have a little sit-down with Luis."

The look on her face told me she definitely didn't envy me. It was pretty similar to the look she gave me when I first shared my impending fate with them.

"Good luck," was all she had for me.

"Can one of you get him on the horn?" I asked.

They had no idea what I had just asked them, I could tell.

"Sorry," I apologized, reaching into my pocket for my phone. "That was evidently white-boy speak for 'can one of you call him for me.'"

With a roll of her eyes, Kiki took the phone from me and began punching his number in. She pressed it to her ear for a second, and then handed it over.

"It's ringing," she said. "He might be a little weird at first, by the way."

"Who's this?" Luis asked. No need for a greeting. I guess this was him being "weird."

"Um, Shawn," I answered.

"Oh, hey, bro," he quickly said. "I didn't recognize your number."

"Oh, yeah, sorry about that," I apologized.

"It's all good," he said. "What's up?"

I was pretty hesitant to tell him, and he wasn't even there with me.

"I need to talk to you about something," I began. "And I really don't think you're gonna like it."

There was an uncomfortable silence for what probably amounted to about a minute.

"Okay," he said. "Hit me with it."

He sounded like he was going to take this better than I thought. In hindsight, this was pretty naïve of me. He had me thinking we were close to being boys.

"The girls don't want to be Destinas anymore," I announced, sort of rushing through it. *I* almost couldn't decipher what I said, and I was the one who said it.

"One more time," he requested. "A little slower this time, though."

I took a deep breath, and manned up.

"The girls don't want to be Destinas anymore. They've made a decision for Jesus, okay?"

"Yeah?" he calmly said. "I mean, if that's what they want. Just remind them, though, that there are rules for leaving."

Such as? I mean, if they were all leaving at once, then who was going to jump them out? Not the *Destinos*? Because that would be wrong on so many levels.

"Okay," I said, still confused.

"*Now*, bro," he continued. "Remind them *now*. And tell them we'll bring the dice."

I cupped the phone even though there really wasn't much point in this measure. Then, I nonchalantly addressed the room, still too confused to feel altogether like the bearer of bad news.

"He wants me to remind you that there are rules for leaving," I said. "And that they'll be bringing the dice."

Immediately, the girls exchanged depressed looks. Obviously, they were all fully aware of what he was implying. At first, they kept me in the dark, but eventually I pressed; I felt I had to.

"Well?" I asked. "What are the rules for leaving? And what's up with the dice?"

I could tell none of them was too eager to share with me.

"Sexual favors," Michelle finally grumbled. She placed her hand on Rosa's knee. "Let's just leave it at that."

Nobody shot her any kind of a glare for speaking out of line. Honestly, I think they were all okay with it because it meant none of them needed to.

Now, I didn't like the sound of this at all. As a matter of fact, *I* decided against it. I brought the phone back up to my ear.

"How else can we make this happen?" I asked. "Because I can't ask them to do this."

"Look, there are only two ways for them to leave. It's either this or they get jumped out," he said, as though he had zero choice in the matter. "And we don't hit females, so…"

"Then hit me," I suggested, without even mulling it over.

"*What*?" he asked, incredulously.

"I'll take the beating for them," I said.

"Bro, you're talking about a beating for *each* of them," he said. "You get that, right?"

"Yeah," I said.

"*What's good with you, bro*?" he asked.

"I thought you were a religious man," I said, foolishly hoping this would somehow get him to switch up his forthcoming plans. "You should get why I'm doing this."

"Just because I know it, doesn't mean I'm always gonna show it," he explained. "Feel me?"

"Yeah," I answered. "But, I mean, with everything that's gone on…"

207

"What?" he asked. "You mean with the whole Angela thing and whatnot?"

"Yeah," I said, surprised this evidently wasn't enough.

"Bro, it's not like I didn't believe in any of this shit before all of this," he pointed out.

This was *not* what I wanted to hear. My reasoning skills were utterly useless here.

"I know, but…"

"Look, where do you wanna do this?" he asked, interrupting me before I could fail to reason with him, once again. Maybe it was a good thing he cut me off, though, because I didn't really have anything prepared. I just didn't want to give up.

"Here, I guess," I suggested.

"At your home?" he asked. "Why am I not surprised? We'll be there in a couple of hours. Keep in mind, if this is a set-up and the boys show up…"

"It's not," I interrupted, slightly offended. "I mean, I wouldn't really be helping the girls any if I did that, now, would I? In fact, I'm guessing that would only make it worse for them in the long run, right?"

He sighed. I really don't think he wanted to do this.

"I hope these chicks appreciate what you're doing for them," he continued. "I mean, there's a good chance you won't be able to walk away from this one; not on your own, at least."

I gulped, and it wasn't for dramatic effect either.

He ended the call, and I simply stared into each girl's eyes – one after another.

Were they really worth it?

You bet your ass, they were. At least, I thought so.

I played both alternatives out in my mind if I didn't go through with this; neither was acceptable. Either they'd turn their back on the Lord for the thug life, which would have been a shame, or they'd pretty much have to subject themselves to sexual slavery, which I'm willing to bet would have haunted me well into my afterlife.

Nope, I had no choice in the matter, as far as I was concerned. At least I'd be able to say I did something worthwhile and noble before I passed on.

After I scanned the room, I discovered Angela standing in the doorway. She looked more appreciative than concerned. Yeah, I was in for what was sure to be one hell of a beating, but I was taking one for *the* team. This couldn't be denied.

A handful of souls would be saved as a result. I mean, really, what more could either of us have asked for?

Kiki stood and approached me. I waited for her to thank me, but she pulled me right in for a hug instead.

I guess this was her version of a "thank you." Some of the others had tears in their eyes, so I can only assume she did, too. Yeah, I definitely made the right choice.

Was I scared? *Abso-frigging-lutely!* I wasn't scared enough to entertain second thoughts, though.

No. I *needed* to do this.

Something good *had* to come out of whatever time I had left. No buts about it. I couldn't leave with any regrets, especially any I might have paid for in my next life.

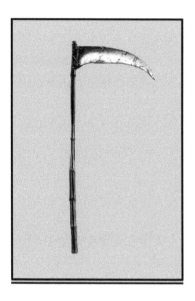

Chapter 17
Angela

I couldn't get over what he was doing for them. I honestly couldn't believe it. God only knew what they were planning to do to him.

I mean, they were a pretty serious gang after all, and I'll bet this was kind of unprecedented. Even if Luis *did* genuinely like him, I doubt he liked him enough to go easy on him because when it came right down to it, they had an image to maintain and word would have definitely gotten around when it came to something like this.

They couldn't take this short. Even I knew that.

I'll be honest. I didn't want him to go through with this. I just couldn't bear to watch it, that's mostly what it was.

I knew he had to die soon, but I didn't want him to come to a violent end.

211

I'll admit it, he was the closest thing to a boyfriend I'd ever had. He felt it, too, I know he did. And I didn't even need to hear his thoughts to arrive at this conclusion.

"Can I speak with you upstairs?" I asked, from across the room.

He nodded, and then gently freed himself from Kiki's hug. She was *so* appreciative.

First, her mother was saved, and now this. She was in Heaven – well, let's just say she seemed happier than I'm sure she ever thought she'd be.

It didn't take long for him to join me in my room. He was nervous, wondering if he maybe should have gotten permission for this first.

"I *am* proud of you," I began. "I'm just scared. That's all."

"Oh, you're worried about me?" he asked, smirking now.

"That's so sweet."

"Shut up," I said, faking a pout. "I'm serious."

He dropped the act.

"I know," he said.

"I'm scared, too. I was just trying to lighten the mood. Look, I know we have something special going on – you and me. You don't have to be a mind-reader to see that. I know you said that business about not being able to have 'earthly desires' way back when, but I can tell we have some sort of chemistry going on here, so who knows?

"Maybe you misheard them or something."

I had the feeling he knew there might be some holes in that whole "no earthly desires" spiel.

"You're doing a very brave and selfless thing, you know," I said.

"I guess so," he agreed, as though he wasn't already fully aware of this. "The way I see it, though, I'm dying anyways, so…"

I suddenly grew nervous. I mean, was he *trying* to off himself?

"What's wrong?" he asked, no doubt noticing my concerned expression.

"This isn't a suicide mission, is it?" I asked. "Because if it is…"

"*It's not!*" he blurted out.

"I would *never* do that. I mean, if you kill yourself, you don't get into Heaven, right? I think somebody told me that once. No. I'm hoping they *don't* kill me. Besides, I doubt they will. I mean, they don't want to risk going to prison over this, so I should be good."

Well, this was definitely a relief. I thought for sure he was up to something the way he was talking.

"Plus, I want it to be you," he added. "Not anyone else, least of all them."

"You want *me* to kill you?" I asked, with my hands pressed to my heart, mocking him; a little payback for earlier. "That is *so* sweet."

It actually was. To be honest with you, I wanted to kiss him right then and there, but I held back. It wasn't his time yet. He still had work to do. I realize that sounds a little cold, but I'm willing to bet he'd have said the same thing.

"Um, do you want to see or talk to anybody just in case?" I asked. I was trying to run down a list of possible loved ones in my mind, but *I* couldn't think of any and none came to his mind either.

"Like *who*?" he asked.

I detected a little attitude, but it wasn't directed at me. Maybe it was for someone who didn't make his list.

"I don't know," I said. "What about your aunt or uncle?"

He did mull it over. Not for very long, though.

"No," he said. "I've pretty much already said my goodbyes to them. And I'm content with how everyone handled it."

"Well then, I guess there's nothing to do now but wait," I said, once again hoping this hadn't come across too cold.

My biggest concern had more to do with his afterlife than anything else. It wasn't where he was headed I was concerned with, but what his role would be when he got there – providing he'd even have one. I assumed they were prepping him for *something*. I mean, he was certainly proving himself down here.

"*I love you, Angela*," he blurted out.

Wow! Talk about unexpected. By this, I mean he must have said it the instant he felt it. I had no prep time whatsoever.

"I don't care if you aren't allowed to love me back or whatever," he continued.

"This is how *I* feel, and I just wanted to get it out there while I still could. You asked me if I had anybody I wanted to talk to just in case, right? Yeah, well, that person is you. You've changed me for the better.

"I'll be honest, before you came along, I believed in the Lord and appreciated the sacrifice He made for me and everything, but He wasn't as important to me as He should have been. I mean, I hadn't written Him off or anything even though the people I loved most in the world were dropping like flies, but I definitely didn't care as much about Him anymore.

"I guess you could say I had my own little Job scenario going on. Except, unlike him, my love for the Lord definitely wavered. You've steered me back, though, so thanks."

I didn't know what to say. I mean, how do you respond to something so poignant? After a brief bout of soul-searching, I responded the only way I thought I could.

"I love you, too."

I suddenly longed to be rebellious; I didn't want to do what I was here to do. I mean, what if I never saw him or felt his spirit again? Could I really risk that?

Unfortunately, I had to, though. My fear of the possible repercussions alone was enough to keep me in line. One for sure weighed heavily on my mind.

Would something like this get me cast out of Heaven? If the punishment was to fit the crime, it should have. Then what? I'd still be without Shawn.

I made sure not to share my internal struggle with him; I couldn't risk him sabotaging his own plan. If I didn't know better, I'd have said Satan was at work here, trying to alter *my* course.

That wasn't possible any longer, though, was it?

Suddenly, for the first time in a long time, I panicked. I definitely needed Michael here with me; he was my security blanket. Alas, though, he apparently didn't feel the need to intervene on my behalf.

This was all on me.

"I think you should be alone with your thoughts for a while," I told Shawn.

"And if I were you, I'd take this time to speak to the Lord."

He nodded, still a little speechless no doubt. I guess I had hit him with a pretty big bombshell.

A couple of hours later, just as it was getting dark out, Luis and the boys showed up.

I expected them to have their usual hood walk going on, but they didn't. I wouldn't go so far as to say they were nervous, but they did, for the most part, have a look of uncertainty about them.

Either they didn't want to run the risk of beating this poor, innocent guy to death *or* they were worried about pissing the Lord off providing they really did believe this angel business was on the level.

I couldn't hear any of their thoughts, so I had no idea where they stood on the topic of me and why I was here.

"Luis," Shawn said, acknowledging him with a head nod.

"Shawn," Luis answered. I was surprised he didn't address him the usual way.

Surprisingly, Shawn took this opportunity to extend his hand. Luis simply stared down at it for a moment before shaking it. He was obviously still struggling with the uncertainty of it all.

"Are you sure you wanna do it this way?" he asked, with concern in his eyes.

"I don't *want* to," Shawn replied.

Luis nodded his head a couple of times.

"You have to," he said. "I'm hip."

"Okay," he continued, looking cautiously around the living room.

"No point in wasting any more time, then. It looks like you've got a lot of nice stuff in here, or at least, breakable stuff, so do you wanna do this outside – in the backyard or somewhere like that?"

"Sure," answered Shawn.

"Okay," he said. "Then lead the way."

Shawn had a very sullen look to him as he took that long walk outside. The girls all stood in silence. They wouldn't even break it for a "thank you" or some words of encouragement.

Then again, what could they have really said to him that their tears hadn't already conveyed?

Luis hung back as the others followed Shawn out back. He seemed agitated with the girls – not for the reason they probably thought, though.

"All of you, outside, *now*!" he barked.

"You owe it to him to watch. This dude is doing something I sure as hell never would have done for you – for *anybody*, really. So, show him the respect he deserves."

Michelle got a little brave. She stepped forward.

"Yeah, well, if you respect him so much, how come you're doing this to him?" she asked. She definitely had fire in her eyes. I kind of expected her to fall back a little after she made her point, but she didn't.

"*Shut up, bitch*!" he shouted. "This ain't even about *you* anymore."

Suddenly, in what was perhaps their most commendable act aside from making a decision for Christ, the Destinas all stood alongside

Michelle. Luis was only taken aback for a moment; his surprise soon returned to agitation.

"Oh, that's cute," he said. "You look more like some white-girl sorority now than a street gang. Good luck out there without us. You'll need it."

"There's no such thing as luck," I corrected him, though he obviously didn't hear me. None of them did, but I really don't think they needed to.

He stormed out of the room, headed toward the backyard.

"*Damn!*" said Rosa. "I hope he doesn't go harder out there now. Maybe you shouldn't have brought the smoke, Michelle."

Michelle looked worried now. Her boldness had finally given way to nervousness.

"I didn't think of that," she admitted. "I sort of got caught up in the moment."

"It wasn't all you, girl," Kiki explained. "We gassed you up a little afterwards, which probably got him even more heated; it had to have."

She shook her head. Clearly, she was frustrated.

"Alright," she began. "Let's just head out there. I mean, Luis *is* right. We do owe him this much."

We all filed out of the living room, en route to the backyard.

By the time we got out there, Luis was well into his rundown of the ritual. Shawn just stood there, listening intently as though he were about to take a final exam or his driver's test or something along those lines. He wasn't fidgety at all, which sort of surprised me.

I'm thinking even the bravest of men get nervous from time to time, and if ever there were a time for him to be nervous, I'd say this was it.

"So, you understand what's going on, right, bro?" Luis asked. "For each of these chicks, except for Michelle, we're gonna kick your ass for *two* minutes. And you can't defend yourself no matter what. If you do, we start the clock again."

217

Shawn nodded. He probably didn't want to answer him in case his voice cracked or something like that.

This was, after all, sort of his badass moment. Fair to say?

"Your only other option, I guess, is if you just wanna get stomped," Luis added.

"*Stomped*?" Shawn asked, breaking the silence he was trying so hard to hold on to. "What's the difference between that and a regular beating?"

Luis eyed Shawn suspiciously.

"I think you're better off with the original plan," he explained.

"This way, we all just wipe you and that's that. The other way, *getting stomped*, is just what it sounds like. A couple of us will hold you down while everyone else takes turn stomping down on your head with our Timbs. That's a lot of damage to the head, bro."

Shawn was visibly shaken; he really wished he hadn't asked.

"I'll just take the beating," he said.

Luis nodded, all business.

"Okay," he said. "Now, remember, try not to defend yourself or we'll need to start all over again. If you want, we can get it all out of the way at once."

He counted the girls, excluding Michelle. "That should take about ten minutes. Or we can break it up into two-minute intervals. It's your choice."

"I'll take them all at once," Shawn said. "I just want to get it over with."

Luis, once again, glanced over at the girls.

"One of you is keeping track of time," he ordered. "If you have to start over again, I'll let you know."

"She won't need to start over again," Shawn said.

He wasn't trying to show Luis up; he was just showing his character, if you ask me.

"Good to know," Luis added. "*Squad up!*"

218

Suddenly, like a pack of wild dogs, they attacked poor Shawn. They punched him relentlessly from all angles until he had no choice but to fall to the ground.

He hoped this didn't count as a defensive maneuver when he landed. This definitely reminded me of the Destinas' assault on me, except mine didn't last long after I went to the ground.

His lasted; they kicked him like crazy while he was down there. I'm willing to bet they even cracked a few ribs in the process.

When they neared what was probably the halfway mark, they helped him to his feet again and started all over – not time-wise, mind you.

Luis connected with two right crosses, sending him to the ground once again.

When he rolled over onto his side at one point, I saw his face – his nearly unrecognizable face. The poor thing. The girls all gasped.

I couldn't take anymore. I rushed over there and tried desperately to intervene, but it was as though they couldn't even feel my hands on them.

Have you ever tried fending off an attacker in a dream and you're getting nowhere with him – like your best punches couldn't possibly affect him in the slightest?

Well, it was kind of like that. I felt like a little three-year-old kid trying to hit a grown man. It sucked. I was frantic now; I wanted to cry, but, of course, I couldn't.

"*Michael*!" I shouted. "Please, stop them! He's had enough."

He was nowhere to be found, though. I should have expected as much. Whenever I thought I needed him the most, he didn't show.

All I could do by that point was walk back and stand with the girls. I felt like such a failure, like I had really let Shawn down.

If only they had been Satan's angels, then I'd have been able to get right in the mix and get him out of harm's way.

When I'd finally had enough and looked away, that's when I first noticed him standing there, just outside of the melee.

He blended in well with the rest of them. The only thing that gave him away was nobody was calling him out for not jumping in.

Luis especially would have been all over this, I think.

I wasn't sure *who* he was here for, but I knew why he was here. I needed to think this over before making my move. It couldn't have been any of the girls because they had all been saved, just in the nick of time possibly.

And the boys all looked pretty healthy and Shawn wasn't planning on fighting back anyways, so...

That's when it hit me! *Shawn* was who he was here for. Judging by my expression, he must have realized I'd figured it out.

Suddenly, he was a bystander no more; he sauntered toward the action.

He was just about in the mix when I grabbed him from behind. I hooked my arm around his throat and began backing him away from Shawn. He was strong – about the strongest I'd dealt with so far.

"Angela," I suddenly heard from the melee.

It was Shawn. He was barely audible, and from the looks of it, barely conscious.

We locked eyes and I couldn't let go just then – not of my hold or my stare. The angel struggled to free himself, but this only prompted me to squeeze harder.

"Angela, please," Shawn pleaded. He wanted me to end it.

Luis noticed this; he stared into Shawn's eyes and then back where we were. Once he must have realized what was happening, he pulled the Destino closest to him away from Shawn.

"Okay, you guys!" he shouted. "That's it! He's had enough."

Kiki blessed herself.

The remaining Destinos all backed away, leaving a bloody and battered Shawn sprawled out on the ground. He was barely moving.

Luis looked about as close to crying as someone like him probably ever had.

"Kiki," he began. "Can you clean him up, please?"

Please? Was this the same Luis? Something powerful had definitely happened here.

"Yeah," she quickly answered. "With what, though? I don't even know what he has in there."

She motioned to the house.

"Not in there," Luis continued. "In the trunk of my car, I've got a plastic bag. There's some olive oil, some wine and a package of bandages in it. Go get it, will ya?"

She was definitely confused, but she hurried around the side of the house anyways.

I wasn't confused, though. This was very familiar.

Luke 10, I believe. "The Samaritan soothed his wounds with olive oil and wine, and bandaged him." Luis was indeed full of surprises.

I shouldn't have let my mind drift from the task at hand, for the angel appeared to be catching his second wind.

Luckily, I still had him around the neck.

I squeezed and squeezed until his struggle ended.

I then cast him off to the side and approached Shawn.

This was it. I'd decided that now was the time to take him. I pulled him to his feet, and held him there. I needed to; he didn't have the strength to do so on his own.

The others must have thought he'd gathered the strength somehow because none of them seemed too freaked out over it – just a little surprised, especially Luis.

He seemed so frail in my arms. They'd whipped him bad; really bad. I brought his lips closer to mine.

"I am *so* sorry, Shawn," I whispered.

Just as our lips met, I felt a sharp blow from behind.

Both Shawn and I fell to the ground. They all rushed over to him, and Luis dropped to his knees.

"*Bro…bro!*" he repeated, lightly tapping him on his cheek a few times.

The angel mounted me and was soon choking me with more force than I think even I had ever exerted.

Who was he?

He was much more of a threat than any of the others – possibly even a few of them combined. I had dropped my guard. Michael was right about earthly desires; they had no place in my life anymore.

Suddenly, something or somebody pulled him off of me. I thought for sure Michael had finally come to my rescue.

I knew a lecture would undoubtedly follow, but I'd have been more than happy to sit through it if it meant I was still in the picture.

It wasn't Michael, though. It was *Shawn*! He was a beast! Not literally, mind you. I mean he was beasting it, absolutely *wiping* this angel.

I couldn't believe it. "How was this even possible?" I thought.

That's when I quickly glanced over to where I had left him, and he was still there, sprawled out on the ground, with the others standing around him and Luis feeling for vitals.

He was dead, and now he was here with me – saving me.

"*He's dead, yo!*" a panicky Luis shouted.

They all quickly shushed him, clearly not wanting to run the risk of finding any of his neighbors up in their business. This wasn't their hood; there's no doubt in my mind it was far less common to hear somebody shout this in Shawn's neighborhood.

At least, I hoped so. I needed to know there were *some* places this plight couldn't spread to.

"I *knew* we went too far," he added. "*Damn!*"

"We had to," one of the others claimed, already making excuses.

"Not really," Luis countered. "If we were in *our* hood, then yeah, but not out here. Nobody would've been hip if we went easy on him out here. Now we might *all* be going down for this."

It was kind of sad that they were once again only thinking of themselves. I suppose this was normal, though.

I should've expected as much out of a street gang. I'd heard about all I wanted to hear and then some, so I checked on Shawn.

"*Shawn!*" I cried out.

He was on his knees, alone and panting. The angel was gone.

Once he caught his breath, he rose to his feet and hurried over to me. We immediately embraced. I never hugged anybody so hard in my life – not even Mama.

"I guess I made it," he said, followed by a nervous sort of chuckle.

"I guess you did," I said.

"You must be Michael," he said, looking over my shoulder.

He gently released me. Then I, too, turned to face Michael.

I swung my arm around my man.

Michael smirked.

"Ecclesiastes 4," he said, shaking his head in disbelief.

"Two people are better than one, for they can help each other succeed," Shawn replied.

"Well done, Shawn," he said. "What do you say you and I take a little walk?"

I released him… and nudged him towards his new boss.

Angela and Shawn will return in *Angela of Death – Iron Sharpens Iron.*
Available September 10th, 2024.
From Watertower Hill Publishing.

Acknowledgments

Thank you to anyone who has ever supported me in my creative journey. Many of you were here at the start of this long trek and others have joined the walk along the way. All of you hold a special place in my heart.

This book is for you and every other reader who loves to get lost in a good story. Included amongst you are my family, my friends, and my newest friends at Watertower Hill Publishing.

Thank you for taking a chance on me.

John Cady was born and raised in Massachusetts. When he's not busy teaching the English Language Arts to juvenile offenders, he's making memories with his family and entertaining readers with his stories.

These stories can be found in multiple anthologies, including After The Kool Aid Is Gone, It's All Fun and Games Until Somebody Dies, ABC's of Terror Volume 3, and The Dire Circle. His debut middle grade horror novella Attack of the 3-D Zombies was published in January of 2022.

This work of fiction was formatted using 12.5-point Times New Roman Font, on 60lb cream stock paper. The page size is 6.14" x 9.21". The margins are industry standard, 1.0" all around, with no right margin, and 0.65" mirrored gutters with no bleed. The cover is full color hardback in a matte finish. The binding is 'perfect.'